C0-ALR-544

Matt lifted my chin and smiled. "Carrie?"

I swallowed. "Yes?" Matt drew me to him, holding me tight. I knew he was going to kiss me. I closed my eyes as his face came toward me, then his lips touched mine.

Caprice Romances from Tempo Books

A CAPRICE ROMANCE

CARRIE LOVES SUPERMAN

Gloria D. Miklowitz

TEMPO BOOKS, NEW YORK

CARRIE LOVES SUPERMAN

A Tempo Book / published by arrangement with
the author

PRINTING HISTORY
Tempo Original / July 1983

ISBN: 0-441-09178-4

Tempo Books are published by The Berkley Publishing Group,
200 Madison Avenue, New York, New York 10016.
Tempo Books are registered in the United States Patent Office.
PRINTED IN THE UNITED STATES OF AMERICA

Chapter One

"Carrie! Carrie? Are you up yet?"

I groaned and snuggled deeper under the covers. It couldn't be time for school, not yet!

"Carrie? Do you hear me?"

"I'm up! I'm up!" I called back, not stirring. There was still time. I could always tell by Mom's voice. First there'd be the friendly but firm calling: the first stage. Five minutes later she'd sound annoyed, very put-upon: the second stage. Finally, when time ran out, there'd be the really irritated, no-nonsense, "You'd better get up or else" cry.

There was time. It was only stage two.

I pulled the covers up around my head so only my nose and eyes stuck out and settled in for those last few sweet minutes before I really had to get up. Settled down to my favorite early morning daydream—Matt.

First, I'd let the picture of him take shape in my head. He was tall and fair-skinned. Dark, shiny hair hung almost to the thick eyebrows that spanned marvelous, dark, mysterious eyes. Now, I moved down his athletic body to his hands. Hands

1

say a lot about people. Mom's hands are square and practical. Dad's are large and capable. My own hands are more round than square, with longish fingers, but not nearly as long as Matt's. Matt's hands are special. Narrow and graceful and sensitive—like an artist's, like a musician's.

Today's daydream began in a new place. The hall in front of Journalism class. I'd be walking briskly to class, knowing perfectly well that Matt strode just behind me with those long-legged steps he takes. Of course I couldn't let him know that, even though my heart would be pounding and my ears tuned to his very breathing only yards behind me.

"Carrie?" he'd ask, loping up to my side and grinning down at me.

"Yes?" Not one bit flustered, I'd offer a friendly, innocent smile to his flushed face.

"I'm Matt Baldwin. I've been wanting to meet you ever since the first day of class."

"Yes?"

"*Carrie!*"

I woke up fast. Glaring down at me, hands on hips, lips pursed in annoyance, was Mom—far into the third stage. I threw off the covers and leaped to a sitting position.

"Do you know what time it is? The bus will be at the corner in exactly twenty minutes. And you said you were up!"

"I know, I know, I was just—" I slipped out of bed and around Mom to the bathroom. Hurriedly, I brushed my teeth and ran water over my face. Pulling a comb through my hair, I took quick in-

ventory. Skin clear today, thank goodness. Mouth
a bit too large. Nose, well—a nose is a nose. Hair,
thick, red-brown, tending to curliness, especially
in damp weather. Eyes, big, and *nearsighted*. I had
to bend very close to see clearly without my
glasses. For two years I'd been pleading for contacts, but all I ever got was, "Someday." Dad said
they cost a lot, and Mom said, "Knowing you,
you'd drop them or lose them within a week."

I stuck out my tongue and made a face. Why
couldn't I have been born cool and beautiful like
my older sister, Lynn. Or irresistibly cute like Pam,
who's only five. I tossed the comb into the medicine chest and skipped back to the bedroom.

"What am I going to do about you?" Mom complained as she darted about the room picking up
yesterday's socks and dirty clothes and a couple of
Pam's toys. "You're fifteen already! When can I
start counting on you to be helpful? When do I get
to do *my* thing?"

"Mom." I closed my mouth. Now was no time to
argue about her unfairness. It wasn't true that I
didn't help around the house. I dusted and vacu-
umed when I had to. I helped with dishes almost
every night—well, when I had to. I took care of
Pam a lot more often than Lynn ever did. I quickly
pulled clean underwear and a T-shirt from the jum-
ble of clothes in my drawer. Darn. If only I could
be neat like Lynn. If you opened her drawer everything would be stacked in tidy little piles. I swear
my sister's got ESP. If I so much as breathe on her
clothes, *she knows*.

"Now, in for breakfast!" Mom commanded. "I

don't want you going off to school on an empty
stomach!"

The lace to one of my sneakers broke. I looked
up to ask Mom if she had any extras around but
changed my mind. She looked so funny, somehow.
Gray and drawn and tired. I'd never noticed those
parentheses around her lips before. They made her
look unhappy. Today she was especially irritable.
In fact, more than just today.

But I didn't have time to wonder. A look at the
clock was enough to send me flying around the
room in search of books, jacket, and purse. Not
sure I had everything, I dashed into the kitchen.

"Oooh," I sank onto the bus seat beside Gayle,
my best friend. "What a morning. I got up only ten
minutes ago. Let me catch my breath."

"I should be so lucky. You know when I got up?
Five o'clock! I was at Dad's over the weekend, and
you know how that is. Monday morning we have to
get up in the middle of the night so he can drive me
back to Mom's in time for school."

"I'd hate that," I said. "Not seeing my Dad every day, I mean. Is it awful?"

Gayle shrugged. "Oh, it's okay, once you get
used to it. Actually, I see more of Dad since the divorce. Before, he was always away until really late
and left before we got up. Weekends he always
seemed to have work to do at the office."

"And now?"

"Now he's around. I mean, I *see* a lot more of
him. Not that we talk more than before. He's usually up on a ladder painting, or under the sink fix-

ing something when I'm there. Daddy and Julie bought this real old house, you know. They couldn't afford anything else after the settlement. It's a pretty busy place the days Danny and I are there, what with Julie and her kids and all that work Daddy does weekends."

I studied Gayle closely. We'd known each other since before junior high. Two years ago her parents decided to separate, then divorce. Gayle took it hard. She'd cry unexpectedly and was always trying to place the blame. "Maybe it was my fault," she'd confide. "Maybe they'd still be married if I hadn't been so mean to Danny last week so Mom screamed and Dad got mad. Or maybe if I'd been better about taking care of Shalimar so Daddy wouldn't have had to walk her each night when he was tired. Or maybe if I wasn't so messy."

"You're always blaming yourself, Gayle," I'd say. "Did it ever occur to you that maybe they just stopped loving each other?"

"If you love somebody, you don't just stop. If that's true, maybe they'll stop loving me and Danny."

"It's not the same," I argued. But I hadn't been at all sure.

For a while I watched my own parents for signs of trouble, worrying they might stop loving each other. But, after a while, I stopped worrying. It was only lately that something seemed different at home. I couldn't quite put my finger on what. Maybe it was all the dinner talk, so much of it between Daddy and "his girls"—Lynn, Pam, and me. Somehow, Mom always seemed to be left out. And afterwards, when the dishes were cleared, Daddy would look at Mom in a strange way, then disappear into his study to work.

I braced myself against the seat in front as the bus rumbled to one of its many stops. I was listening to Gayle complain about being so far from her friends the weekends she spent at her Dad's, when suddenly she looked surprised and her words ended lamely in mid-sentence. "Don't look now," she whispered, poking me in the arm. "Guess who just came on?"

"Who?" I turned to look. "Oh, no!" I hid my burning face in my hands and slid down in my seat. "It's *him*!"

"What's he doing on this bus?" Gayle whispered, trying to peek between the seats to the back without getting up. "He's with Robert," she reported. "They just sat down." She got up and pretended to adjust the window so she could see better. "They're talking. He just took an apple from his bag. He's eating it." She sat down. "Maybe he stayed overnight at Robert's."

"Oh, shoot. What'll I do?" I cried. The poised Carrie of my daydreams just didn't exist. If Matt were to sit beside me right now, all I'd be able to do would be to smile. No, not even smile. I'd simper, like a silly junior high baby.

"Think of something else," Gayle offered helpfully. "Think about Journalism. It's Monday. What word are you putting on the blackboard today? Carrie?"

I stopped shaking and tried to focus. For a second all I could picture was Journalism class, where

I sat in the second seat of the first row and Matt Baldwin sat in the next to the last seat in the last row. And then I suddenly realized what I'd forgotten. It was on a lined sheet between the pages of the book on etymology I'd gotten from the library, on the desk in my bedroom.

"The word!" I cried. "I left it on my desk. I won't remember what to write! And it's first period!"

"Come on now," Gayle prodded. "Calm down. You'll remember. Now, what was the word?"

"I don't know!"

"Sure you do. Come on, concentrate."

"I can't! Oh, how could I be so dumb! I *always* forget something. If it's not my lunch, it's a book, or my purse, or something! I hate myself!"

Gayle put a hand on my arm. "You didn't forget. It's all there in your head. All you have to do is picture it. Now come on. It's in that book you showed me. Which word is it?"

I sat straighter and bit my lip. Every Monday in Journalism class, as Lady High Commissioner of Etymology, I was supposed to write a new word on the blackboard. Then I had to get up and explain how the word came to be. The Lord High Commissioner of Lexicography would write an unusual word and its definition on the blackboard. And someone else would write a new proofreading symbol for the class to memorize.

"Tantalize! That's the word. Tantalize! I remembered!"

"Okay, good. And what's the story behind it?" Gayle asked.

"It's coming, wait. Yes. It's from Greek mythology. There's this brutal king, Tantalus, who was condemned to Hades for his crimes."

"There!" Gayle cried triumphantly. "I told you you'd remember."

"Oh, thank goodness. What would I have done? It would have been so embarrassing."

We entered the school grounds, and students began crowding into the aisles even though the driver insisted they remain seated until he came to a stop. Now that I felt relieved about my Journalism assignment, I could concentrate again on Matt. If we didn't rush to get off maybe we could slip into the aisle just in front of him. Maybe he'd recognize me, say something, like in my daydreams.

When I stood up my heart began thumping, and all the blood rushed to my face. Matt was coming down the aisle, head turned to Robert behind him. If he so much as looked my way I was sure to faint. Gayle raised an eyebrow in sympathy and went out into the aisle.

Just as Matt came even with the seat behind, I excused myself and slipped between him and the person in front. It was the closest I'd ever been to him. In Journalism class he sat five rows away. The only time I really got to look at him was when I got up to explain the origin of a new word. As students pressed forward and I didn't move, Matt bumped against me. I closed my eyes to let the whole wonderful feeling seep in. What if he put his arms around me now and buried his face in my hair?

"Hey, you up front! You dead or something? Come on, move up!" I opened my eyes to see

Gayle way at the front, ready to step off the bus—
and a big empty space between us.

Mortified, I rushed down the aisle, nearly dropping my books. Only when I reached the bottom
step did I glance back. Matt, just stepping to the
ground, was looking straight ahead, his thick, dark
brows knit in deep concentration. I fell in step beside Gayle and let myself face the awful truth.

Matt Baldwin didn't even know I was alive.

Chapter Two

As soon as I reached Journalism class I put down my books and went to the blackboard. Jeff Wicker had already written out his new word and definition in a big, sprawling hand. Halley Segal broke a chalk as she underlined something to show the new proofreading symbol. It wasn't until I sat down that I noticed the three names on the left side of the blackboard: my name, Halley's, and *Matt Baldwin's*.

"What are those names for?" I whispered to the girl to my left. "Do you know?"

She shrugged. I was about to ask the boy behind me when Mr. Hawkins stood up. "Okay, Jeff. We'll start with you. What's our Lord High Commissioner of Lexicography got to offer today?"

This was the part that always got me the most nervous. Waiting my turn to stand and face the class made my legs shake under my desk. My face would get hot even before I stood up, and I'd have to clear my throat three times before anything came out. How did anyone ever become confident enough to talk in front of a class?

"Seminal," Jeff said. A small snicker went through the classroom. I wondered if the word had anything to do with sex.

"Of, relating to, or containing semen or seed," Jeff said without the slightest twitch of embarrassment. "Of, pertaining to, or having the power of origination." He paused. "An example, used in a sentence, might be: The president's idea was of seminal importance."

"Good, Jeff," Mr. Hawkins said. Then he called on Halley, who had written on the board, "This is the *word*."

"The way to show you want to italicize a word is to underline that word in the text, then write 'ital' in the margin so the printer can't miss it," Halley said without even standing up.

I wrote it down in my notebook under proof-reading symbols, just as I'd copied the word seminal onto my New Words page.

"Okay, next. The Lord, pardon—*Lady* High Commissioner of Etymology, please."

This was the awful and wonderful moment. I stood up slowly, turning to face the class, and looked directly at Matt. Though I always tried to look elsewhere, there was only one person I spoke to—him.

I cleared my throat. "Tantalize," I began. Matt glanced up from a book he was reading and our eyes met. I almost forgot what to say. "A long time ago in Greece there was a very cruel king named Tantalus. He was condemned to torture in Hades for his terrible crimes. His punishment was to stand in water, and when he tried to drink, the water receded. And, and, there was fruit hanging above him. Whenever he reached for it, it was pulled away." By the time I sat down my palms were damp, my mouth was dry, and my legs felt like wet noodles.

"Carrie, give us a sentence using the word," Mr. Hawkins said.

I jumped up again. "Uh . . ." I cleared my throat. "It's tantalizing to be in the same room with . . ." I nearly died as I realized what almost came out. I took another deep breath and tried again. "Uh, it's tantalizing to be in the same room with, uh, a hot fudge sundae when you're on a diet." I finished the sentence in a rush and let out my breath. Oh, boy!

Mom was always saying, "People shouldn't say the first thing that comes into their heads, Carrie." She was right. "Think before you speak." Right again, but how do you manage that? I usually say exactly what I think two seconds before my brain cancels the order.

Matt's lips formed a crooked grin and he returned to his book. I slid down in my seat with a sigh of relief. One more week and the privilege—in my case, the ordeal—of being the Etymology expert would pass to someone else.

For the rest of the period I concentrated on the class assignment, to write a lead for a story in the text. Only now and then, pencil in mouth, did I look up at the blackboard. I wondered why my name and Matt's were listed.

"I'm sure, as good newspeople," Mr. Hawkins said a minute before the bell rang, "you're all wondering what the three names on the blackboard mean. And, if you haven't wondered, you don't belong in journalism, because one of the most important qualities of a reporter is curiosity. Curiosity, drive, and resourcefulness—the ability to get answers when the usual routes are blocked."

The bell rang, and students started gathering up their papers. Mr. Hawkins held up his hand. "Just another minute, please. We have three vacancies on the *Chronicle* staff. Uusally, we fill vacancies at the beginning of the term, but since the term is almost over, I've decided to fill them now. Carrie, Halley, and Matt, you will report to the *Chronicle* office after sixth period. See Dave Roth, the editor-in-chief. He'll fill you in on your duties."

"Hey, congratulations, Carrie!" someone beside me said.

"Luck-y!" someone else said.

I staggered out of the room in a happy daze. Mr. Hawkins thought me good enough to make the *Chronicle* staff! I couldn't believe it. Me, a reporter! And Matt, too. Just like Lois Lane and Clark Kent. Oh, boy! A grin started in my mouth and spread like a giant rainbow through my whole face.

Immediately after last period I raced up to the third floor and the *Chronicle* office. I'd passed it a zillion times before and always glanced in, wishing. Sometimes I'd see a staff member bent over a typewriter at a table against the wall. But most of the time the kids seemed to be just hanging around. They'd be sitting on a desk edge, maybe, and eating lunch, or talking and joking with each other.

I'd always dreamed of being on the staff, but it seemed hopeless. To make it as a *Chronicle* reporter you had to be most of the things I'm not. Smart and dependable, resourceful and organized. Particularly organized.

As I fought the going-home tide I felt more than a little scared and unequal to the job. Mr. Hawkins must surely have made a mistake in selecting me. Halley and Matt, I could understand, but me? No.

I stopped at the door to the office and peeked in. Neither Matt nor Halley had come yet. A pretty, blonde girl sat on the edge of a table swinging her legs and talking to a boy across the room.

"Excuse me," I said in the most timid of voices. "I'm looking for Dave Roth. I'm supposed to meet him here at three o'clock."

"Dave just stepped out. Be back in a minute," the girl said, then turned back to the boy.

I waited at the door, not sure whether to come in or stay in the hall. After a moment the boy said, "Hey, have a seat. No use waiting outside."

I walked in, clutching my books tight to my chest, and took the closest chair. The girl and boy went on talking as if I wasn't there. Seniors, probably, I thought as the talk bounced back and forth about the most recent basketball game. Sports never really interested me unless I was playing, so I tuned out and looked around.

The room was small, with a teacher's desk at one end, three typewriters on a long table, files, cubby-hole mail boxes, a phone, and a bulletin board just behind me. I twisted around to read what was on it and saw a marked-up copy of the most recent

Chronicle, an assignment chart, school notices, and notes from staff members to each other. Soon my name would be on that board. Carrie Dubov, girl reporter! Maybe I'd even get a by-line. The possibility made me smile.

"Hi, Lisa, Bob." Matt sauntered into the room and dropped his books on the table like he felt completely at home. My heart immediately began doing double time. He nodded my way without the slightest sign of recognition. Then he ambled over to the coffee pot and poured himself a cup. Soon he joined in the talk about basketball.

I wished Matt had thought to offer me some coffee, even though I hate the stuff. But then I thought, what's wrong with you kid? This isn't the Middle Ages. You expect to be waited on? While I was debating whether to get up and get some coffee, Dave Roth burst into the room with Halley at his heels. "I think that's a great idea, Halley," he threw back over his shoulder.

"Sorry I'm late," he announced, picking up some sheets from a box on the desk and glancing through them. He leaned against the desk, made a few changes on one of the pages, then threw them back in the box. "Okay, guys. Let's get down to business. Lisa, Bob. Here's our new staff. Halley," he nodded toward Halley, who smiled broadly from her perch on the typewriter table. "Matt you already know, and uh . . ." He fished around in a pocket and pulled out a folded note, but before he could open it I said timidly, "Carrie."

"Right, Carrie." Dave nodded at the blonde girl. "Lisa is features editor and Bob is sports.

They like to use the office for their social headquarters."

Lisa made a face, and Bob started gathering up his papers.

"Unless you have something better to do than yak about the game last week, make yourselves scarce so I can brief these guys, okay?"

"Yes, sir!" Lisa clicked her heels together and saluted smartly. "Come on, Bob. We know when we're not wanted." She yanked her purse over her shoulder and winked at Matt. "Tough guy, that Roth. Eats nails for breakfast. Glad you made sports, Matt. See ya." She tossed her head at me, and Lisa then tugged on Bob's shirt to get him out faster.

I glanced at Matt. He was watching Lisa disappear, a small, amused smile on his lips. Who could blame him for admiring what he saw? Lisa's jeans fit like skin. Her blonde hair bounced around her shoulders like in a shampoo ad on TV. She was not only pretty, but smart. Sighing, I looked back at Dave Roth.

Squarely built, with brick red hair, he sat on the edge of the desk studying us. He's tough, I decided, noting the crossed arms and no-nonsense look.

"I hope you three realize what an honor it is to be chosen for the *Chronicle* staff before the regular term begins," he said. "But don't let it go to your heads. The honor isn't due so much to your charm and brilliance as to our desperate need. We lost three reporters last month to transfers and dropouts. Our dropout rate's about fifty percent, for two reasons. Some guys think I'm too tough, and some think they can be Woodward and Bernsteins without putting in the effort. The truth is somewhere in the middle. I do run a tight ship, but I also admire and reward talent and hard work." He scratched his head and ran a hand through his hair.

"I have a few rules. One. You turn your assignments in on time, and no excuses. Two, if you're given a story, you cover it whether you want to or not. No excuses. Three. You don't use the office as a hangout. Four. You do check in each day for assignments, or whatever. The whatever includes going to the printer or staying late to proof or type something. Got that?"

The three of us nodded. Matt had separated himself and gone to sit on a high stool near the coffee urn. Halley sat on the typewriter table swinging her legs, eyes brightly fixed on Dave. I was the only one on a low chair. It made me feel small and insignificant.

"Okay. Any questions?"

"Yeah," Matt said. "How long's this coffee been brewing? Tastes like burned glue."

"Sorry 'bout that. By this time of day it is pretty awful. We considered going to instant, but no one wants the responsibility for keeping things clean. You want the job? It's yours."

"No thanks!" Matt replied quickly, holding his hands up in mock horror. "Actually, I'm very fond of burned glue."

Dave smiled. "Yes, Halley?"

"I have a few ideas I'd like to talk over with you. When you have a minute," she said.

"Stick around after. Uh . . ." He referred to the slip of paper again. "Carrie?"

I hadn't expected to be called on. When I found everyone looking at me, waiting for an answer, I couldn't think. I pushed my glasses up. "Uh, uh, when will we get our first assignment?"

"Eager beaver, huh? Well, if you really want to get going, here." Dave reached for a stack of stories in the box on his desk. With a red pen he marked each first page. Then he passed the sheets on to me. "Write headlines for these. I've indicated how many lines I want and how many letters on each line. M and W count as one and a half each. Lower case L and T go as a half, in case you didn't know."

I took the pages with shaking hands.

"Any questions?"

"Uh, no."

"Not even like when it's due?"

"Oh." I giggled nervously. "When?"

"How about tomorrow, by noon."

"No problem." Three little headlines. Shouldn't be hard. I looked down at the pages so Dave wouldn't see my red face.

"If there are no more questions, that's it. See you guys tomorrow. Halley, stay a minute."

I picked up my books, tucked the stories inside my loose-leaf notebook and left the room. What an idiot you made of yourself, I thought angrily, going down the hall to the stairs. At home you hardly ever shut up. With Gayle, your mouth goes about a hundred miles an hour. The one time you really want to make an impression, you can't think of a single interesting thing to say. And what do you say when you do speak? You volunteer! Only kids trying to score with teachers do that. What would Matt think?

Chapter Three

I heard footsteps approaching behind me, just like in my daydreams. Suddenly, there was Matt in step beside me. I glanced up, then away.

"Got yourself some extra work for tonight, didn't you?"

"Oh, I don't mind," I said. "Writing headlines is kind of fun, like working crossword puzzles, sort of. It shouldn't take long."

"Good. You can do my headlines then. Condensing a whole story into two measly lines, including a verb, isn't my idea of fun."

Matt's dark hair fell over one eye, and I wanted to reach up and push it back. He smiled. What did he mean about my doing his headlines? Did he mean we'd be seeing a lot of each other? "Sure," I said. "I'd be glad to help."

He laughed.

Something about the tone made me stop. "What's funny?"

"You."

My face got hot again, and my glasses fogged up. "Why?"

"Well," Matt looked at me in a half-serious, half-playful way and cocked his head to one side. "You're so serious. So intense. You act like being on the *Chronicle* is the most important thing in the whole world."

I stepped back. "It is, to me."

"Oh? I couldn't care less."

"Then why did you join the staff?"

He pushed the dark strand of hair from his eyes. "I love sports. Being on the sports staff I get free tickets to all the games. How about you?"

"Me?" My voice squeaked. "I want to be a reporter someday on a big city newspaper."

"Oh, one of those."

"One of those—what?"

He laughed again. "See? There you go getting serious again. Life isn't *Hamlet*. It's *All's Well That Ends Well*. It's *A Midsummer Night's Dream*."

"What's that?"

"Shakespeare. What are you, a sophomore? You'll get him next year, but read him now. You'll see what I mean."

We walked down the stairs and out the hall to the school exit. I wanted to keep the conversation going. Maybe Matt would offer to walk me home. "What do you think of Journalism class?" I tried.

"It's okay. Better than regular English, where they'd have us diagramming sentences and analyzing Ivanhoe until we'd dissected him to death."

Matt seemed so smart. He read Shakespeare before he had to and actually liked *Ivanhoe*!

We reached the street and stopped; now he'd go.

There was no way to hold him longer. "Well, good-bye I guess," I said.

"You have that look on your face again."

My hand flew up to my hot face. "What look?"

He chuckled. "Most girls don't blush."

"Oh, stop it!" I turned away, almost ready to cry.

"No, really. I'm not criticizing you. It's a compliment. I think it's sort of nice, blushing. Kind of innocent and sweet." His dark eyes looked right into me.

"What look did I have?" I asked.

"The same one you had in Journalism class when you got up to give that sentence on tantalize."

"Oh!"

"What were you going to say, anyway, before you came up with that sentence about hot fudge sundaes? You said, 'It's tantalizing to be in the same room with . . .' With whom? With what?"

"I don't remember."

"Too bad." He grinned at me. "I had a feeling the rest of *that* stuff would have been *really* interesting."

I swallowed. He was teasing again. All those daydreams each morning where Matt and I talked and I acted so aloof while he felt awkward—they were just that, daydreams. Now that we were actually talking, I felt as naive and vulnerable as a baby.

"I have to go. Bye," I said.

"Wait!" Matt called, coming after me.

"What?" For a second I thought maybe he'd ask to walk me home.

"Nothing. Just, see you in Journalism. And don't work too hard on those headlines."

I wanted to come up with some clever answer like Lisa might have, but Matt rattled me too much. Instead, that dumb blush spread over my face again. I turned away quickly so Matt wouldn't notice and almost ran down the street towards home.

"Shakespeare?" Lynn exclaimed. "*You* reading Shakespeare—when it's not assigned?"

Right after dinner I'd settled down on my bed in our room to read. The dusty, thick Shakespeare with the deep blue cover came from the top shelf of my parents' bookcase. I blew the dust off the top and opened the cover. Inside I found Mom's maiden name and the year 1961.

"Why shouldn't I read Shakespeare?" I challenged, flipping through the tissue-thin pages.

"Because, dear sister," Lynn said, peering at herself in the vanity mirror across the room as she applied eye liner, "Shakespeare is for literate people, not morons. In case you don't know what literate means, get the dictionary."

"I know what it means!" I shot back. "Just because you're in junior college doesn't mean you know everything!"

"True, true." Lynn pulled the corner of her right eye. For a moment she didn't speak as she carefully drew the dark liner. Then she straightened up and with half-closed lids turned to me. "Have you ever read any Shakespeare? It's like reading a foreign language. You have to develop an ear for the way the people talk."

I'd already reached that conclusion from the few strange lines I'd tried to read as I flipped through the pages. Frankly, I like to read these long romances where the girl falls in love with a cold, handsome, rich stranger and she thinks he hates her until the end, when they fall into each other's arms.

Still, if Matt liked Shakespeare, then so should I, no matter how hard or boring.

After a few minutes I closed the book and reached for my notebook. Better get to my homework and the headlines. Then I noticed what Lynn was doing. She was applying perfume, dabbing it behind each ear, on her neck and wrists and in the crook of each arm, smiling at herself. I guess I've seen her do it a zillion times, but this time I really paid attention. It had always seemed so fake, putting on perfume and making up your face like you'd do a paint-by-number canvas. What was wrong with the real you? But now I figured maybe she knew something I should know.

"Where are you going?" I asked.

"With Jay. For a drive." Lynn flashed me a bright smile.

Jay has been Lynn's boyfriend longer than anyone else. I really don't know what she sees in him. He's so flashy and boastful and loud. But I guess there's no accounting for taste. "Lynn?"

She tied a scarf around her neck. "Umm?"

"How do you get a boy you like to like you?"

"Make him notice you."

"How?"

Lynn caught my eye in the mirror. "By looking attractive. For instance, you could do something about your hair."

"What else? How do you talk to a boy? What do you say?"

"Flatter him."

"How gross. That's so calculating!"

She swung around to face me. "It may seem calculating, but that's how it works. We read an experiment in Psychology that proves it. A group of women students were told to be nasty to a group of men students. Pretty soon the men just hated the women's guts. Then, the women were told to be nice, to tell the guys how smart they were, how handsome and so on. Before you knew it the men were falling in love with the women."

"Yuck," I said. "What else?"

Lynn went to the dresser and lifted out a perfectly folded sweater in a plastic bag. "Find out what his interests are and learn more about them. Ask him lots of questions. You'd be surprised how interesting a man thinks you are when all you do is get him to talk about himself."

"Oh, Lynn!"

"Oh, Lynn what?" She slipped the sweater over her shoulder and put the plastic bag back in her drawer. She smiled at her image in the mirror.

"Well, you can't really mean that. Men aren't that dumb."

"I didn't say they were, but they do like to be told how marvelous and charming they are, just like we do." She blew an air kiss at me. "Jay doesn't like me to be late. Tah-tah."

My sister disappeared through the door. I sat on my bed, legs crossed, thinking. If I wanted Matt to notice me, to like me and ask me out, that meant I'd have to change my ways. It wouldn't be easy. Clothes weren't something I thought a whole lot about. Sports, unless I was playing, bored me. When I felt comfortable with people, I liked to say what I thought instead of sitting back and throwing questions at them like an interviewer. Still, if that's the way it was done, maybe I should give it a try.

I jumped off the bed and went to the vanity table. Lynn had everything: eye liner, shadow, mascara, blusher, lip gloss, powder, perfumes, and more. All neatly arrayed. Sitting down, as she had just done, I took off my glasses and leaned forward. Pathetic. Then I studied Lynn's arsenal of weapons, picked up the purple shadow, and unscrewed the cap.

"For heaven's sake, Carrie! What's wrong with your eyes?"

I'd come into the kitchen for breakfast the next morning with most of the eye makeup from the night before still intact. As intact as makeup can be when you've washed your face without wetting the area around the eyes. True, some of the liner had smeared, but I'd wiped that away, or most of it. I thought, in fact, that I looked quite sophisticated, at least two years older than I really was.

"Have you been playing with Lynn's makeup?" Mom demanded, coming at me with a wet towel.

"For heaven's sake! Do you want to start a war? You know how she is about anyone touching her things!" Mom rubbed hard under my eyes.

"But Mom!"

"Don't 'But Mom' me. Go inside before Lynn sees and wash that stuff off. And hurry!"

"Mo-ther!"

Too late. I jumped at Lynn's hysterical scream and darted off to the bathroom. I locked the door and turned on the water. Even above the noise of the tap I could hear Lynn's screams. "I'll kill that stupid kid. I swear, I'll kill her! Where is she?"

I leaned against the bathroom door, listening. What was so terrible about borrowing a little of my sister's makeup? How could anyone be so stingy? When Pam grew up I'd let *her* try my things, my makeup and perfumes and even my clothes. I searched in the medicine cabinet for some baby oil, like Lynn used to take off her makeup. Water didn't work so well on the liner. No wonder all those ads said you could wear it even when swimming.

"Car-rie!" Lynn was pounding on the bathroom door. "You come out of there this minute! I've told you a thousand times not to touch my things! Now you're going to get it!"

"I'll pay you back!" I called. "I'll pay you back for every tiny bit I used!" How had Lynn found out? I'd put each bottle and pencil and tube back exactly as I'd found them.

Lynn pounded harder. "You leave my things alone, hear me! You stay out of my clothes! You stay away from my cosmetics! You stay out of my life!"

"Girls, girls, please!" Mom shouted.

"If you two don't stop screaming immediately," Dad shouted, "I'll put you both over my knees and really give you something to scream about, no matter how old you are!"

The pounding stopped; I held my breath and listened hard. Did I dare unlock the door yet?

"Carrie?" Mom called. "Come out of there. You'll be late for school."

"Not till Lynn goes away," I answered.

"Lynn?"

This time I heard movement. My sister's footsteps faded as she went back to our room. Cautiously I unlocked the door and peeked out. The coast was clear. I ran into the kitchen, grabbed my books, and fled down the hall before she could attack me again. How could anyone share a room with a perfectionist? I'd just never get along with my sister!

Chapter Four

As soon as I reached school I raced up the stairs to the third floor to put the stories, with their head-lines, in the *Chronicle* office. I'd stayed up nearly until midnight working on them. I counted letters in each line of each headline until my eyes hurt. It hadn't been so easy, after all. But now, as I put the finished work in Dave Roth's box, I felt good about myself. My first assignment finished. On time, no excuses. Just what Roth wanted.

"Well, what have we here," Roth said, coming into the office just as I was leaving. He dropped his books on the desk and reached into his mailbox. I stayed, waiting. The bell wouldn't ring for another minute or two, and I could hardly wait to see the admiration on his face, hear the praise for my good work.

He reached for his red pencil. "You can't split a verb in a headline," he said. "Do this one again."

I peered over his shoulder. He'd corrected the headline I'd worked on the most, the one I thought perfect. "Ski Club To," would go on the first line, and "Hold Meeting," on the second. There was no way to write that headline in twelve letters or less on each line without splitting the verb!

"And this one," Roth said, marking up my second headline, "has no verb at all. Can't write a headline without a verb."

"But, but—"

"This one wouldn't be half-bad if you'd written fifteen characters per line, not sixteen. How's the printer going to squeeze sixteen letters into a space meant only for fifteen?" He looked up.

"I worked on those headlines for nearly four hours!"

"I don't care how long you worked on them. Work some more. Bring them back tomorrow, written correctly."

"But, Dave!" I cried. "It can't be done. Really! You absolutely can't tell the point of the story on the ski club in so few letters! There's just no way to write that dance headline in fewer than sixteen letters. I tried!"

He stared me down, completely unsympathetic. "There *is* a way; there is *always* a way. You just haven't found it."

I didn't move. He was wrong.

"Carrie? That's your name, isn't it?"

I nodded.

"Well, Carrie, I'm going to give you your first and most important lesson as a reporter. Never, absolutely *never*, say 'can't.' Erase it from your vocabulary. Believe me, there's always some way to do anything. If you get stuck, you just back out and try another way. Got it?" He held the papers out.

"Got it." I took them. "I'll have these back tomorrow." My throat tightened, and the words sounded funny. I turned and rushed out to the hall to my first class, Journalism.

At lunchtime I wrinkled my nose as I entered the crowded, noisy cafeteria. Today was particularly bad. A wet snow in the morning made the room smell of damp parkas and wool caps, plus the usual dirty mop water, grease, mayonnaise, and onions. Maybe a little ammonia. Picturing those things made me want to puke.

Today, I sniffed and pushed back the queasiness, bought a container of milk, then looked for Gayle. We had an arrangement. Whoever got to the cafeteria first would save a place for the other.

"Carrie! Over here!" Gayle's voice rose above the low roar of lunchtime noise. I headed to her table and squeezed in at the end of the bench in a space held by Gayle's books. I pulled my lunch from my daypack.

"What have you got today?" Gayle asked, watching.

"Sardines. Yuck. Mom knows I hate the smell." I pushed the sandwich away. "Nothing's gone right today!"

"I'll trade you," Gayle said. "I've got cheese. Plain ordinary American cheese. Mom says she can't go shopping until payday, or until Dad's support check comes. So it's cheese all this week. Yesterday I made it with mustard. Today, with mayonnaise. Tomorrow, if we have any, I'll add tomato." She lifted the top slice of bread on her sandwich and stared at it without enthusiasm.

"Here. I'll take cheese for sardines any day." I laid my sandwich down on Gayle's baggie. "If *I* made lunch, I'd do something interesting."

"Like?"

"Bacon and tomato. Roast beef and cheese. Like—"

"Don't, please! You're making my mouth water! So tell me. What went wrong today?"

"Everything." I talked with my mouth full, something Mom always says I shouldn't do. "First, Lynn sounded off about my using a speck of her makeup. Then, my headlines weren't good enough for Roth. And then, in Journalism, Matt acted like he hardly knew me, even after yesterday when we had this long conversation and he practically asked me to help him write headlines!"

"Poor you," Gayle said. "If you want to hear a real hard luck story, listen to me."

"This cheese is hard. How long was it in the refrigerator?" I asked.

"Forget the cheese. Are you listening?"

"Sure, what?"

"Last night we had a 'guest' to dinner—a man."

"So? Your mother's been divorced for a year. She has a right to invite a man over."

"Not a man. A kid!"

"A kid?"

Gayle frowned. "I bet he's no more than twenty-one. My mom's thirty-six!"

"Oh." I tried to visualize what it would be like if my parents divorced and Mom went out with men. I didn't like the idea one bit. It would be so strange seeing her with anyone other than Dad! And a guy, only twenty-one! I knew just how Gayle felt. Trying to make her feel better I said, "Men go out with women who are ten, even twenty years younger than they are."

"They shouldn't. What could they possibly have in common? They just do it because it makes them feel macho being seen with a female young enough to be their daughter."

"But if men do it, why shouldn't women?"

"Because. It's practically indecent. Thirty-six, and she's got wrinkles around the eyes. What could he see in her?"

"I don't know. Maybe he likes her personality."

"He's practically my age. He's hardly lived. What can she see in him?"

Chemistry? Maybe that was it, but I didn't say so to Gayle. She looked miserable enough. I chewed the dry cheese sandwich and washed it down with milk. "What's he look like? Is he a jock?" I asked.

"Broad shoulders, narrow hips and a big smile." She shuddered.

"Sounds gorgeous to me. What's he like?"

"Okay, I guess."

"So what's the problem?"

"The problem is, he's not my father!" Gayle whispered angrily. "I don't like him telling me what to do. Can you imagine, he had the nerve to say I shouldn't eat and talk at the same time! And he's only six years older than me!"

"What did your mom say?"

"She sat there with a smile on her face like she'd just discovered heaven."

"What did you say?"

"I said I'd eat the way I wanted to; it was my home and he should mind his own business. And then Mom said, 'Gayle! That's fresh! Ned's my guest and you're being rude. Apologize or leave the table.'"

"You left the table."

"You bet!"

"Gee, Gayle, I'm sorry. That's really tough."

"I tell you, Carrie. If Mom starts seeing a lot of that creep, I'm gonna pretend he doesn't exist. I won't open my mouth at dinner, or I'll just eat by myself!"

"Maybe she won't see him again," I offered.

"She will. I could tell by the way she looked at him."

"Well, then, maybe you'll get to like him somehow."

"That'll be the day."

Right after last period I rushed up to the *Chronicle* office. Maybe, if I was lucky, Matt would be there too. Maybe I'd find my name on the assignment sheet with some juicy story to cover. Maybe some of the other reporters would be around and would want to talk.

But, except for Lisa, the office was empty. Lisa sat at a typewriter, working. She glanced up for only an instant, nodded, then went on with her work. I dropped my books in a corner and went to the coffee machine. In every movie I've ever seen about reporters, they always brought coffee to their desks. Maybe with a cup in hand I'd look official. "Lisa? Want some coffee?" I asked, dropping three heaping spoons of sugar in my cup to disguise the taste.

"Uhm, uhm," she replied without turning.

"Is that yes, or no?"

"No!" She went on typing.

I made a face at her back and wandered over to the bulletin board. The assignment sheet hadn't changed since yesterday. But on the board was a notice I hadn't seen before. It said:

Attention Staff:

We always need good features. Don't only count on being assigned a story—show some initiative. I'm always looking for good ideas. Either propose them to me, or go on and write them and take your chances. How about a feature from each and every one of you?

Lisa

My head started buzzing with ideas. What could I offer? Cruising! Lots of the kids cruised in their cars down Main Street on Wednesday nights. I'd never done it, but maybe I could hitch a ride with someone who did and write, "Cruising Main Street—Fun and Trouble." Maybe there wouldn't be any trouble, but then again . . .

What about divorce. Half the kids in the school came from divorced families, or so the rumor went. Maybe I could interview Mrs. Moffat, the school psychologist, and come up with some ideas on how to handle special problems. In fact, maybe I could start a column, a kind of "Dear Carrie," to deal with problems of divorce.

And what about interviewing that neat kid in my French class, the one always doing card tricks and disappearing acts? He once said something about training to be a magician. Could I do something on that?

"Lisa?" I could hardly wait to get her reactions.

She didn't answer.

"Lisa!"

"For heaven's sake, be quiet! Can't you see I'm trying to concentrate?" Lisa put one hand on each side of the typewriter and glared at me.

"Oh, I'm sorry."

"Well, what is it?"

"Never mind; it'll wait." All of a sudden I couldn't stand the bitter coffee, but there was no place to throw it. The cup was still half-full. I downed the rest like you'd drink poison, and shuddered, throwing the cup away. I picked up my books and started for the door.

"Hold on. You might as well sit down and tell me what you wanted to say. I've lost the thought, anyway!" Lisa said.

I hesitated. She made me feel so inexperienced and dumb, just the way my sister made me feel. I no longer had any enthusiasm for talking about my ideas.

"I'm sorry I growled at you like that," Lisa said. "It's just that I have a deadline. This stuff has to be at the printer's by five. I've got two features for the next issue of the *Chronicle* that need complete rewrites. Now, tell me what you wanted to say."

"Just some ideas about some features, but I'll wait till you're not so busy. Can I help? Type something, maybe?"

"I wish, but thanks anyway. This is something no one else can do." Lisa looked back at the paper in the typewriter and chewed her lip.

I got up quietly and left, calling out softly "Bye." Her hand went up in response, but she didn't reply.

Leaving the office I almost bumped into Matt. My heart began its usual thud-thud beat. "Hi," I said.

For a second it seemed like Matt didn't really know who I was. Then he said, "Oh, hi. How's it going?"

"Great!"

"Good," he said, passing me. He started to whistle.

I waited in the hall as Matt entered the room, expecting to hear Lisa explode at his distracting noise. But all I heard was Lisa's warm, friendly voice saying, "Hi, Matt. Have a seat. Be with you in a sec."

Chapter Five

I had just finished setting the table for dinner when Mom came in from the kitchen. "You can put one setting back," she said. "Your father isn't coming home for dinner tonight."

"Daddy isn't coming home?" I got a tingly, scared feeling up and down my arms.

"Right," Mom said. She busied herself at the buffet, her back to me.

"How come?" I asked. "Mom? How come? He never misses dinner!"

"He had work to finish at the office. Now do as you're told and call your sisters. It's time for dinner." It was odd how Mom didn't look at me and her voice sounded hard and cold.

"Let's wait, hunh? We'll eat when he gets home," I urged. Gayle's remarks about the late hours her Dad kept just before the divorce came back to me. I figured if we all waited till Dad got home, then ate together, everything would be fine.

"We'll eat without him, Carrie. Please do as I told you."

"When is he coming home?"

41

"For heaven's sake! Stop it! You never let go! You're like a dog with a bone. You just never let go! How many times do I have to tell you?"

"All I asked . . ." I didn't finish the sentence as Mom stalked out of the dining room to the kitchen. I followed. She opened the oven, donned an oven mitt, and lifted the foil from a casserole. I waited in the middle of the room not knowing what to do. What did it mean? Was something wrong between Mom and Dad?

"Are you still here?" Mom asked, turning. She put the steaming casserole on the counter and hung the mitt on a hook. "Don't you listen?"

Trembling, I fled before she could say more. In the dining room I removed the water glass, napkin, and silver from Dad's usual place and put it on the buffet where we could get it in a hurry. Then I went to call Lynn and Pam.

"And you know what that dumb boy did?" Pam bubbled as she forked up a chunk of chicken and pushed the peas aside with one finger. She had started talking the moment she sat down. Daddy's absence hadn't been noticed at all. "You know what he did?" she repeated. "He jumped right into the sandbox. And he stepped right on my sand castle. And he smashed it right to bits."

"Eat your peas, Pam," Mom said.

I caught Lynn's eye and motioned to Mom. She seemed a zillion miles away. Just before dinner I'd told Lynn of my suspicions, but she'd only laughed. "There you go again with that crazy imagination of yours. You ought to be an actress the way you make a big drama out of every little thing."

Lynn gave me an annoyed look and turned her attention to Pam. "So, what did you do, Pammy? Did you give him a good whack?" she asked.

Mom cleared her throat. "I have something to tell you girls," she said.

Uh-oh. Here it comes, I thought. My legs began to shake, and I felt a terrible need to go to the bathroom. "Excuse me, please," I said, getting up.

"Carrie, can it wait? I have something you should hear."

There was no escaping. I sat down again with the certainty that now she'd say it. They were going to get a divorce. Life would never be the same again. I swallowed the lump in my throat and hid my cold hands in my lap.

"As you may realize," Mom began, twisting the gold chain at her neck around a finger, "I've been pretty testy lately." She gave us all a weak smile. I wanted to reach out and touch her.

"I've been short-tempered and irritable, and you must have been thinking I'm going through the change." Mom's lips trembled. "Well, I'm too young for that, and I'm too old to be hanging around the house all the time being the chief cook and bottle washer."

"But, Mom," Lynn interrupted. "You're more than that. What about the volunteer work you do?"

Mom shook her head without much conviction. "I have to look ahead. You girls are getting older. Soon Carrie will be off to college, just like you, Lynn. College costs money." She smiled. "With you two gone, what will I do with a big house and no one in it?"

"You'll still have Pam and Daddy," I said.

"Yes, of course." A little pulse on Mom's neck began beating faster, and she covered it with one hand. "Well . . ." She let out her breath.

Here it comes now, I thought. Oh please, don't. I closed my eyes a moment, then opened them. Mom was watching, a small, uncertain frown on her brow.

"What I've decided to do, have done in fact," she said, eyes still on me, "is get a job." She looked uncertainly from me to Lynn and Pam.

"A job?"

"You're surprised? Yes, at the bank."

"At the bank?" So that's what it was all about! Nothing at all about divorce. I was so happy I jumped up and hugged Mom. "Why that's wonderful!" I cried.

"I'm so glad you don't mind!" she said. "I thought you girls would be upset. I was pretty good at math in college, you know, before I married your Dad. I only dropped out when I got pregnant with Lynn."

"Well, I'm glad it was only a job," Lynn exclaimed.

"Why? What do you mean?" Mom asked.

"Your darling daughter Carrie has been building up an epic scenario about you and Dad, divorce, that kind of thing. She almost had me thinking . . ."

"Why, Carrie!" Mom gave me a searching look.

"Well, you know . . ." I gave her an embarrassed grin. "Divorce is kind of like the flu. Everybody seems to be catching it."

"Not us though," Lynn said. "I told you."

Mom shook her head. "What I wanted to talk about is how my working is going to change things around here."

"What changes, Mom?" I asked. Pam was muttering something about hating peas. I'd suspected for some time that it wasn't the vegetable she didn't like, but the name for it. "Pam," I said gently. "Why don't you eat those lovely green balls, honey? Green balls are delicious."

"Oh." Pam put a pea in her mouth and tasted it uncertainly. Then she smiled.

"What changes, Mom?" I repeated.

"Well, for one, you girls will have to help more. You'll have to get used to getting yourselves up on time, getting your own lunches, keeping your own rooms clean, helping with dinner, things like that."

"Oh, that'll be easy," I said.

I called Gayle right after supper. The only way I can ever get privacy on the phone is to take it from the hall into my bedroom and shut the door. Even then someone could pick up the kitchen extension, or Lynn's liable to walk in.

"Guess what?" I said as soon as Gayle came on the line.

"By the tone of your voice, it's something good. Did Matt the Superman ask you out?" Ever since I told Gayle about the Lois Lane–Clark Kent image I had of Matt and me, she'd been calling him Superman.

"Not yet, but I'm working on it."

"Then what?"

"Mom's going to work starting Monday."

"What's so great about that? Wait till you have to do the laundry and everything else."

"Don't you see? All that worry about my folks' acting weird was nothing. It's just that Mom's gotten restless and ambitious. She's even talking of becoming bank manager, and she's only starting as a teller!"

"I hate to disillusion you, Carrie, but just because she's taken a job doesn't mean a thing. My Mom got a job two months before she and Dad separated."

I gripped the phone tighter. "Oh?"

"Yeah. I guess she saw the handwriting on the wall. With Dad living elsewhere it would cost more—where would it come from? So she went to work."

"That's not what's happening with my parents!"

I could almost see Gayle's stubborn, freckled face as she pondered her answer. "Probably not," she said finally.

"Not probably. Absolutely!"

"Right. Now let's talk about something else. Did you hear about Midge's party Saturday? She invited just about everyone. I offered to bring a dip."

"Am I invited?"

"Of course. She knows you and I are best friends. You can bring chips or colas or something."

"Did she actually say I was invited?"

"Well, no," Gayle said hesitantly. "But you know how it is. Word gets around and everyone just comes."

I hated pushing in where I wasn't invited. Midge and I hardly knew each other. She was a year older, drove a car, dated a senior, and knew just about everyone in school. "I don't know," I said at last.

"Now you listen here, Carrie Dubov. You're going to that party with me or I won't go. Rob's going to be there, and Matt's a friend of his, you know."

"You think Matt might come?"

"You'll never know unless you come."

Lynn marched into the room. "Are you still on the phone? Jay said he was going to call, and you've been on that phone since dinner. Now get off!"

I turned my back on Lynn and curled into the receiver. With the door open I could hear the TV from the family room and Mom reminding Pam in a stage-two voice that it was bedtime.

"What did you say, Gayle? Lynn just walked in."

"I said you'll never know if Matt comes unless—"

"Will you get off that phone?" Lynn repeated, hands on hips, directly in front of me. "You can talk to Gayle tomorrow. You're not the only one in this house, you know."

"Mom!" I shouted, holding my hand over the mouthpiece. "Mom!"

Gayle was going on about what she would wear

and how neat it would be if the two of us could double-date with Robert and Matt, but it was hard to concentrate.

"*Now* what's going on?" Mom stood at the door, frowning. "Can't you two get along for three minutes?"

"The brat won't get off the phone!" Lynn complained.

"She has no right talking like that when I'm on the phone!" I cried.

"Stop it, both of you! Lynn, act your age! And Carrie, make it short. Lynn needs the phone."

"Gayle, I gotta go," I said. "The witch wants to hear from her *amour*."

I hung up and stuck my tongue out at Lynn. "It's my room too." I dropped down on my bed and kicked off my sneakers. Almost immediately, the phone rang.

Lynn grabbed for it. In the sweetest, gentlest voice you ever did hear—the kind she never used at home—she said, "Hello?"

This lively, happy, warm and charming person was my nasty sister? I did a double take. Love transforms.

As soon as she realized I was listening, she gestured wildly for me to leave. When I didn't go she covered the mouthpiece and hissed, "Out, out. Hear me?"

I made a disgusted face and very leisurely slipped my sneakers back on, then ambled out of the room. She shouted after me, "And close the door!"

* * *

Reworking those three headlines wasn't easy, believe me. I sat at the kitchen table for two whole hours trying to think. I even used the thesaurus. I stretched my mind as far as it would go, got up and ate an apple, then stretched some more. Finally, I saw what was wrong with the ski headline. I was hung up on using the words Ski Club as part of the headline. Once I realized that, lots of other possibilities opened up. For instance, I could say "Skiers Plan/Next Outing." That added up to ten letters on each line and said what the story was about. Roth should be delighted.

Just as I began packing my papers away, Mom came into the kitchen. She went to a drawer, took out a tack and then went to the bulletin board near the phone. The board is always full of junk: old shopping lists, Pam's scribbles and drawings, family snapshots, telephone numbers and so on. For a while Mom stood there looking at the stuff. Then she began unpinning nearly everything. When the board was almost empty, she tacked a sheet right in the middle of it.

"What's that?" I asked, going over to look.

"See for yourself."

It said "Schedule." Under it were four columns, for Mom, Lynn, me, and even Pam.

"I've got to be at work by eight," Mom explained a bit apologetically. "So I won't be able to get you guys up or take Pam to school. I figure Lynn can set up the breakfast things—she's always up and organized early. You can make lunches."

I studied the list more carefully. All the things she had always done were being unloaded on me and Lynn. Especially me.

"I'll still do the shopping, which is a big job, and make most of the meals," Mom went on. "But things like cleaning up and washing the laundry—"

"But Mom," I protested. "I've got school and homework and the *Chronicle* now."

"I know that. And Lynn's got school and homework, plus her part-time job, plus Jay. And your father's too tired to do much. And Pam's too young to be of much help. So who's to do it? I'll be gone eleven hours a day!"

"Must you work?"

"Yes, I have to work." Mom's tone was quite final. "You'll notice the schedule starts tomorrow, instead of Monday. I need a few days to pull things together, get a working woman's wardrobe, stock the pantry, that sort of thing."

I stared glumly at the sheet. Tomorrow I was expected to set the alarm and get myself up. No more extra minutes in that wonderful half-awake, half-asleep state when the best daydreams came. It was my task to make lunches for Pam and me. Then I had to see that she got off to kindergarten, just a block away. After school, it was up to me to pick Pam up at Valerie's, bring her home, keep her happy, set the table and put dinner in the oven. Nice. Just because Lynn was at school all day fooling around with Jay she got away with murder.

"You'll notice that Lynn serves dinner and does cleanup," Mom said, reading my thoughts. "I worked on this a long time, trying to be fair." She stopped me before I could protest. "Give it a chance, honey. Please?"

I hated it. Hated having to do dumb housework when I'd much rather be reading or hanging out with friends. I hated not having Mom around when I got home from school because it was the one time—I'd grab a glass of milk and a cookie while she fixed supper—that we could talk. I hated it. A lot of good that did.

Mom's look was so sad and anxious and hopeful at the same time that all my anger turned to love. I walked over to her and hugged her tight and nuzzled my face against hers. "Sure, Mom. I'll try. I really will. Honest."

Chapter Six

I hadn't seen Matt in three days. I don't know where he kept himself. Everyday I'd pop into the *Chronicle* office after lunch, during free period, after school, just to kind of look around. To find Matt, really. But not once did I catch him.

On Friday I thought—I hoped—maybe today. Right after my last class I hopped up to the third floor. But first I stepped into the rest room. For lunch I'd made myself a fantastic sandwich— pepperoni and mortadella cheese on french bread—yum. Fantastic, but lethal. You never know with pepperoni. It can leave a smell on your breath that reaches across a football stadium. If the taste in my mouth was any sample, I'd better go home, I thought. So, before going to the *Chronicle* office, I had to check. I breathed into my cupped hands and sniffed. Things seemed okay. I popped a mint, just to be sure, and nervously headed down the hall.

"You type?" Roth asked as soon as I came into the room. The small office looked busy, with two typewriters working, someone arguing with someone else, and a couple of people bent over galleys.

Actually, I may be the fastest pick-and-peck typist in the school. I learned on Dad's machine and tried to mend my ways by taking a typing course during the summer after eighth grade. But three weeks into the course we all went on vacation. Back to pick and peck.

"Here. Type this up. We need it fast," Roth said. "Halley? What've you got?"

It was just a routine story about the Math Club. Nothing interesting. I finished it and took another. The second story was handwritten in a hard-to-read, tight script. It was about the new basketball coach. Normally, I'd be bored stiff, but this story had style. "With an easy lob Coach Wilson hurled the ball halfway across the gym directly into the basket. He plugged platter-sized hands into a green Lincoln High parka and talked, not of basketball, but of warm, sunny days and purple sunsets in California."

By the time I reached the last paragraph and turned the page, I was wondering who the author could be. The name started with a printed M and then became kind of a long-trailing nothing with a line above the nothing, like the crossing on a T. Matt? The thought brought excited chills.

"How's it going?"

Matt's voice came so unexpectedly that I jumped. Sweat trickled down my arms, and I took my glasses off because they got all steamy. Dangling them by their frames, like they do sometimes in movies, I gazed up at Matt.

"Is this yours?"

"Sure. Why? Don't you like it?"

"It's good! It's great! I love it!"

He smiled and touched my shoulder. "Thanks. Sorry you got saddled typing my stuff. I better take typing soon. You really gallop along there with only two fingers."

I nodded and gave him the pages but kept my face as far away as possible so he wouldn't smell the pepperoni. "What's that word?" I asked.

"Erudite."

"Erudite. Oh, sure." I smiled like I knew what the word meant and turned back to the typewriter. With Matt looking over my shoulder I started making mistakes.

Roth handed me a third piece to type after I turned in Matt's. As I rolled the paper into the typewriter I tried to hear what he was saying. "Good stuff," he told Matt. I stopped typing and pretended to read the copy. "But cut the purple prose. You're writing news copy, not a literary masterpiece. And keep the words down to two syllables. How many kids in our school know what erudite means, for instance? What's wrong with something simple, like wisdom, learning, or even know-how?"

"What's wrong with educating them?" Matt asked.

"The average person reads at about fourth-grade level, Matt. Remember that." Roth scribbled something on top of the page. "You'll get a by-line for this one. How do you want it, Matt or Matthew? And give me a headline. Three lines, fifteen letters per. Go to it."

I wondered if Matt would ask me to write the headline for him, but he went off to a corner to work. When I finished the typing, I went to the bulletin board to see if any new assignments had been put up. After all, Matt was getting his first story published, so what about me?

Lisa had posted a couple of ideas for some of the older staff to check out. Halley was down for an assignment, but there was still nothing for me. Did Roth forget who I was, or did he only want me for my typing?

Disappointed, I wondered what to do next. I could go home, but I wanted to hang around. How else would I get to know the other reporters? How else would I get to know Matt?

"Whoever isn't doing something directly connected with putting out this next issue, go home," Roth announced. He seemed to be looking directly at me. Everybody seemed to get busy working, except me. I picked up my books.

Roth waved a hand my way. "Thanks for the typing, uh, er, eh . . ."

"Carrie."

"Oh, right."

I glared at him, but his back was already turned. Dave Roth, I vowed silently, you're going to know my name by the end of this term, and that's a promise! I glanced once more at Matt, who bent over his story, working on the headline. So much for rushing to the *Chronicle* office in hopes of being noticed.

Since I stayed late, I missed the school bus and had to walk home again. It's almost three miles, so by the time I got to Valerie's house to pick up Pam, it was almost five o'clock.

"You're supposed to be here by three!" Pam cried in greeting. "I'm going to tell Mommy!" She pounded on my stomach and sounded close to hysteria.

"What's wrong with you?" I asked, holding her off. "Now stop that!"

"Pam dear," Valerie's mother said while her daughter stood by, thumb in mouth, looking anxious. "It's all right. Really. I told you she'd come." She stroked Pam's hair and spoke soothingly. "She's tired. It's all so new and strange to her. And of course it is a long time for such a little girl to be away from her own house. She'll get used to it. But she's afraid."

"Of what?"

"All change scares these little ones. She was afraid you wouldn't come. Now that your mother's away all day she's afraid of being abandoned. Who knows what goes on in their heads?"

"I didn't realize." I took a tissue from my purse and wiped Pam's eyes. "Come on, sweetie. I'll take you home. I'm sorry."

We walked home together with Pam sniffling, but holding my hand. While I made small talk about her morning at school and what she did at Valerie's, I worried. How could I be active on the *Chronicle* if it meant staying late after school? I'd always miss the school bus. Then I had an idea. Much as I hated the thought of biking to and from school, I'd have to. That way I could get home faster than on foot. My old bike sat in the basement, its tires probably flat. I'd have to try to get it working.

When we reached home I gave Pam her favorite doll and told her to put it to bed. "She's missed you all day, Pam. Why don't you lie down with dolly until dinner time so she'll feel safe."

With Pam at rest I checked Mom's instructions for dinner. I was setting the table when the doorbell rang.

"Gayle!"

She stood at the door grinning, hands behind her back. "So? Don't I get invited in?"

"Of course! Come in! But it's almost dinner time. How come?"

She followed me into the kitchen, sniffing. "Beef stew, right?" She sniffed some more. "No, something else, but it is beef."

"Meat loaf surprise," I said.

She sat down, hiding something behind her. "What's the surprise, that it goes for three meals?"

"Fun-ny. No. There's applesauce in it and chunks of cheddar cheese." I giggled. "And it probably *will* go for three meals. The way Mom plans food these days, it's one for the table and two for the freezer. What's that behind your back?"

Gayle sat up like a proud peacock. "Guess."

"Ah, come on. I hate guessing games." I poured two glasses of apple juice and brought them to the table. "What is it?" I tried to grab what she held behind her, but she wouldn't let go.

"It's a surprise, for you. As soon as I heard you'd made *Chronicle,* I thought of it. It had to be made up." She brought a paper bag out and removed a nicely wrapped box. With a big smile and a flourish, she handed it to me.

I put my juice glass down and wiped my hands on my jeans. A present for me! Only Gayle would think to do something like that. Carefully, I removed the yellow ribbon and tried to undo the tape so it wouldn't tear the pretty paper.

"You shouldn't have," I said, fingers fumbling with the box. Then I lifted the lid and tore through the tissue inside. Underneath was a bright pink T-shirt. On its front, in bold black letters, was written *Writers Are Novel Lovers*.

"Oh, Gayle!" I squealed. I put my hand over my mouth as I got the point.

"It's you."

"You're crazy!" I laughed and hugged her. "It's wonderful. I love it!"

"I knew you would." She looked pleased. "Now put it on."

I slipped out of my long-sleeved plaid shirt and pulled it on. It fit snugly, like a bathing suit.

"That should get super-Matt's attention. I bet Lisa'll wish she had one."

She followed me to the bedroom where I could stand in front of a mirror. We both stared at the image.

"It's my favorite color," I said. "But look how big it makes me look in front."

"All the better."

"Gayle, I can't."

"Oh, come on, Carrie. Don't be a square. If you think it's too tight, just put your hands inside and stretch it. You're so used to wearing these blouses and loose tops. Haven't you noticed? Lots of girls wear Ts that tight."

"It's not that."

"Then what?"

I covered my face with my hands. "It's embarrassing, what it says. I haven't got the guts."

"Oh, come on," Gayle said. "I never even thought . . ."

"How could I face Matt or anyone at the *Chronicle,* wearing this? But Gayle, please don't be angry. I love you for thinking of me."

"Well, what's this?" Lynn had come in while we were in the bedroom. She looked at my shirt and grinned. "Cute!" She hung up her coat and put her books neatly on the desk. "Oh, that is fun-ny!"

"Yeah. Well, would you wear it?" I asked.

"Who gave it to you?"

"Gayle."

"Very clever, Gayle." She shook her head. "A little premature, though."

"Which means?"

"To be a writer you have to have written, and as far as I know you haven't written anything yet, anything that's publishable. That's number one."

"And number two?" I crossed my arms over my chest to hide the words.

"Number two. You haven't even dated, so how can you qualify as a lover?" She ran a brush through her short, soft hair.

"Nothing like a big sister to give one confidence," I said. I pulled the shirt off and put my plaid back on. "Gayle, let's go inside."

Gayle looked disappointed when I put the shirt back in the box. But I couldn't honestly promise to wear it. I'd die of embarrassment. "Maybe later," she said as I walked her to the door. "Maybe when you're really in solid at the *Chronicle* and feeling real good about yourself you'll wear it. Huh?"

I hugged her for her thoughtfulness. "Maybe," I said to make her feel better. But the truth was, I couldn't imagine ever having that much confidence.

I spent a lot of time getting ready for the party at Midge's Saturday night. Mostly on my hair. Usually my mop looks clean enough, but thick and kind of untamed. The smallest breeze tosses it about so that any style I may start out with disappears. What I hoped to achieve was a soft, sophisticated look. With my tight, new jeans and the emerald green crepe-de-chine blouse I got for Christmas, I hoped to look smashing. Maybe Matt, if he came, would take note.

"Come here," Lynn said, eyeing me critically. "Let me see what I can do. Sit down."

I sat in front of her dressing table, and she took me in hand. She swooped my hair behind my ears, then lifted it on top of my head, then brushed it back and forward. Finally, she took out her curling iron and curled it back, away from my face.

"Not bad," she said. "Now, for the eyes."

She put a touch of green eye shadow on my lids, enough liner to make my eyes look really big, and two coats of mascara. The effect was really nice. It made me look kind of oriental.

"That's nice, Lynn. Not like me at all," I said, leaning closer to the mirror to see better. "Thanks."

Lynn cocked her head to the side and smiled. "You're not as ugly as I thought. Here. Put on your glasses. See how it looks."

I put my glasses back on and stared in the mirror. The effect was spoiled. Back to old four eyes.

"I will not wear these things tonight!" I said, tossing my glasses on the dressing table. "For once I want to look pretty!" With all the eye makeup and no glasses, my eyes felt funny.

"Put them back on," Lynn said. "It's not that bad. You're practically blind without them."

"No! If I can't have contacts, then I'll just do without when I go to parties. It's bad enough I have to wear them at school."

"If you want contacts so badly, get yourself a part-time job and earn them," Lynn said.

"Maybe I will!" I reached for my coat and went out to the living room to wait for Gayle.

Dad looked up from the newspaper and gave me a long, low wolf whistle. I stood straighter.

"I hope she can tell the boys from the girls tonight," Lynn said, giggling when Mom asked about the glasses.

Fortunately, Gayle arrived. "Now remember," Mom said. "Curfew is midnight. Call your father and he'll pick you up. And Gayle? Better let Carrie hold your arm. She can't see more than five feet in front of her."

"Mom exaggerates," I said, closing the door behind us. I took Gayle's arm. "But just the same . . ."

Chapter Seven

Gayle's Mom dropped us off at Midge's house. I got all fluttery and excited and scared as we went through the front door. A line of balloons hung from the entry ceiling. Bright colored paper hands with thumbs pointing down a hallway led to a door and the stairs to the playroom in the basement.

Midge's Dad had made over the basement so it looked like the inside of a ship, with fishing nets and harpoons tacked to the wall. The lighting wasn't much. At the far end of the room spots lit up a Ping-Pong table where four kids were playing and others hanging around.

Most of the activity took place in the darker area. A nice fire blazed in the stone fireplace, giving off the only light to the dance floor. Chairs and couches had been pulled away from their usual places and set against the walls to clear the space. An old jukebox blared forties music and lit up one corner. Most of the kids were dancing where it was darkest.

"Munchies are always welcome," Midge said, leading us to the snack table where she put out

Gayle's dip and my colas. She showed us where to leave our coats and then we were on our own.

"See anyone we know?" I asked Gayle over the music. Without my glasses everything seemed slightly out of focus.

Before Gayle could answer, someone came up and tapped her on the arm. "Hi, Gayle. Want to dance?"

"Oh, hi, Rob!" Gayle said, somewhat breathlessly. "Sure." In a moment she went off on Rob's arm, leaving me with an encouraging smile. I don't think Rob recognized me.

On my own, I wasn't quite sure what to do. I ambled over to the snack table and admired the variety, but really didn't feel hungry. I poured a glass of punch just to look busy, then stood against the wall with my drink, tapping a foot to the music. I wished someone would talk to me or ask me to dance.

After a minute or so I wandered to the far end of the playroom where the Ping-Pong players were. Where was Matt? If Robert came, shouldn't Matt be around?

A lot of the kids had moved away from the table. Only a half-dozen or so hung around, watching. One was Matt. My mouth immediately went dry. I edged over to stand beside him and sipped the drink, pretending he wasn't there.

"Way to go!" he yelled as one of the players made a good shot.

"Yeah!" I joined in.

"Tough slice!" he called.

"Neat play!" I echoed.

He noticed me then and smiled.

"I used to be pretty good at Ping-Pong," I said. "Beat everyone in my family. Even my dad."

"No kidding? How about the next game?"

"Sure, why not?"

"By the way, I'm Matt," he said.

He didn't recognize me. Because it was dark? Because I didn't look like me? "I'm Carolyn. Carrie for short."

His head swung back and forth as he followed the play. Hearing my voice, hearing my name made no impression.

Before long we stood at opposite sides of the Ping-Pong table smiling at each other, paddle in hand.

"For ups," Matt started the ball easily, and we passed it back and forth three times. On the fourth turn, I sliced the ball and Matt missed. I was up.

I should have beat him. He had a steady game without any surprises. When I play Dad, I like to lob and slice and sometimes slam the ball low over the net to the farthest corners. But I couldn't see well enough, even squinting, so I lost, 21–15.

He came over afterwards and put his paddle down near mine. "You play pretty well, for a girl."

"For a *girl*!"

He laughed as if he'd said that just to see my re-action. "Say, you look familiar. Do I know you?"

I blinked at him through heavy eyelashes.

He scratched his head. "Are you in my Physics class?"

"No."

"French?"

"No."

"Hmm. Somehow, I thought I knew you. Oh, well. Want a drink?"

I held up my half-full glass and shrugged.

"Dance, then?"

"Why not." I put my glass down and let him guide me to the dance floor. I couldn't believe myself. The new me, created by Lynn, appeared so self-assured. The real me felt quite the opposite. Inside I was shivering so hard it took all my efforts not to show it. I hoped the perspiration running down my arm wouldn't ruin my new blouse.

Matt, hand at my back, steered me smoothly to the dark end of the room. Kids were dancing to a velvet-voiced man singing "Night and day, you are the one . . ."

"That's Frankie," Matt said.

"Oh?"

"Frank Sinatra. He's great, isn't he?"

I really wasn't a big Sinatra fan, but I agreed. To tell the truth, I didn't really hear much of what Frankie sang, or what Matt said. I was too busy tuning into my feelings. Matt put his right hand on my shoulder and took my damp left hand in his. For an instant we faced each other waiting for the beat, eyes locked. He smelled clean, freshly laundered, with a faint scent of lime. His dark eyes sparkled in the flickering firelight, and I closed mine for an instant, feeling weak.

My heart must have been thumping two hundred beats a minute as we waited. As we moved together, I tipped my face so my cheek touched his. My face burned. My legs trembled. I could feel his heartbeat against my chest, strong and fast.

"You know," he whispered in my ear after a time, "I still think I know you."

You should, I felt like saying, but the Carrie who might have said that wasn't this Carrie. Instead, I laughed a small, throaty, mysterious laugh, the kind I imagined Lisa or Lynn might have given. And Matt held me closer.

Next Monday, when I came into Journalism class, I wondered and hoped that Matt would know me. But, with makeup gone, glasses back on and hair only a vague imitation of how Lynn had fixed it, I looked my old self. My sister was right. Boys judge you by the "packaging" first. Apparently I'd been packaged right, because Matt wasn't the only boy I danced with. He wasn't the only one who asked for my phone number.

I settled into my seat and rummaged through my books for the word to put on the blackboard. Then I casually turned around to sneak a quick look at Matt. Hands behind his head, he stared up at the ceiling, off in some other world.

All during the time I was explaining the origin of the word sinister, I felt his eyes on me. Dark, brooding eyes, just like those of heroes in romance novels. I stumbled over the explanation and finally sat down, trembling. When the bell rang, I practically flew out of the room.

Matt caught up with me at the stairs. "You're Carrie, aren't you?"

I stopped, angry now. "Oh boy!"

"What's wrong?"

"According to Hawkins, reporters are supposed

to be sharp. They're supposed to be good at re-
membering names and faces, that sort of thing."

"So?"

"So—yes! I'm Carrie. You've heard my name
every day for weeks now when Mr. Hawkins calls
on me. You met me in the *Chronicle* office. We
talked in the hall. We . . ." I almost said that we'd
danced together at the party but stopped myself.
"Yes, I'm Carrie. Glad you finally remembered!"

I started walking, fast. With his long legs Matt
had no trouble keeping up. "You're angry," he
said.

"Sure I am. Why shouldn't I be?"

"You're angry because I didn't recognize you at
the party."

He knew. He did know who I was. My face
flushed, and I could have killed myself for letting
him see my reaction.

"I didn't really figure it out until this morning
when I looked at you. Even with the glasses, I
knew. It's the way you talk."

"What's wrong with the way I talk?"

He took a step back. "Hey, don't bite me! I gave
you a compliment! It's your enthusiasm I noticed,
like I did Saturday night."

"Oh!" I took a deep breath. "Oh."

"Even if you're not a very good Ping-Pong
player."

"Not a good Ping-Pong player? Oh yeah? I could
have beat you with one hand behind my back if—"
I stopped. He was trying not to laugh, and I realized he'd been teasing me. I'm so used to de-

fending myself against Lynn's snide remarks that I just reacted normally.

"You'd have beat me if what?" Matt asked.

I opened my mouth, then closed it. Lynn said you should make the guy feel superior. What difference could it really make if he thought he could beat me? "Oh, nothing," I said lamely.

The second bell for next period had already rung. We each had classes in opposite directions. "Well, see you around, Lois Lane," Matt said, grinning.

I did a double take. Did he have the same fantasy I did? "See ya, Superman," I said.

Gayle and I met for lunch and compared notes about the party. She really liked Robert and thought he'd be calling her. I told about the newest developments with Matt, and we plotted how we'd arrange to double-date sometime in the future.

"*If* he calls," I added. "Now that he knows the party Carrie is plain-Jane Carrie in Journalism class, he probably won't."

"He'll call," Gayle said. "I just know he will."

At the next table I spotted Bill Westkopf. He's the guy I had thought about writing a feature on when I had read Lisa's notice. Bill had been at the party, too. He'd performed some neat magic tricks, and I'd thought again about doing a story on him. We'd all gathered on the floor, facing the fireplace, and Bill had put on a show for about fifteen minutes. He'd pulled scarves out of his sleeves and unknotted a rope that had a big, firm knot in the middle simply by passing his hand over it. And he kept up a line of funny jokes; I guess it's called patter.

"Gayle, excuse me a minute, will you?" I said.

She gave me a questioning look, but I slipped off the bench and tapped Bill on the shoulder. He had a mouthful of egg salad when he turned around. "Justh a min . . ." he said, gulping fast.

"Bill? I'm Carrie. Carrie Dubov? Remember? I met you at the party Saturday?"

He recognized me immediately. "Yeah, sure. You're the girl Matt danced with so much, made me jealous."

"Oh, come on," I said, blushing. "I didn't dance with him that much. I mean . . ."

"Hey, sit down." He made a space for me, but I didn't sit.

"I really came over to ask you . . . I mean, I'm on the *Chronicle* staff. A reporter, you know? And I wondered if I could interview you sometime? Do a feature on your magic act?"

"Sure!" he said immediately. "I'll take any publicity I can get. Just say when."

"When?" I laughed. I'd never asked anyone for an interview before, and I didn't seem to be coming across very well. "How about after school today? Wait, no. I've got to pick up my sister." For a second I thought of asking him to come to my house, but that sounded very unprofessional. "Friday, in the library, about three?"

"Got a better idea," he said, reaching up to my hair and taking something out of it. "My goodness! An egg." He showed it to everyone at the table.

"How would you like to come to a magic show Friday night? My Explorer Scout troop's putting on a Court of Honor. Everyone's into magic, and we can talk then."

All the time he was speaking he was doing something. The egg he had taken from my hair went into a pocket, and he took another egg from behind my ear. "Are you a chicken?" he asked very seriously. "You seem to be laying a lot of eggs!"

Everyone at the table, in fact everyone in the cafeteria, seemed to be laughing. I laughed, too, but I could hardly wait to go back to Gayle and kind of fade back into the woodwork. He wrote down where I lived and said he'd pick me up at seven-thirty Friday evening. Then I left.

"You've got a date!" Gayle said.

"It's an interview, not a date."

"He's cute. Don't you think so?"

"Yeah, he is," I said. Then I realized he really wasn't. Actually, he was kind of thin and not very tall, and his complexion wasn't very good. But at the party, when he performed, I'd thought of him as pleasant looking, tallish and well built. It's funny how a nice personality makes even ordinary people seem beautiful.

Chapter Eight

Thursday afternoon we had a staff meeting in the *Chronicle* office. The new issue had just come out and would be distributed to the whole school on Friday. Meanwhile, we each took an advance copy and were asked for comments.

As soon as I got my copy, I looked for the headlines I'd written. Two of the three were printed just as I'd turned them in the second time. The ski headline had been changed.

"Looks good," someone said, breaking the silence.

"You think so?" Dave tapped a pencil on his finger. "Let's see. On page one I count four typographical errors. Why? Either you guys can't spell, or you didn't proofread the page. Who gets the credit for that sloppy job?"

A guy in front of me put his hand up half-heartedly.

"Okay, then, let's move on to the editorial page. Any comments?"

"Isn't everybody sick of reading about trash

pickup? Didn't we do that subject a month ago?" one of the girls asked.

"Right, we did, and the problem is still with us. I'm just as bored as you are with it. So? How about finding something original to give us your opinion on for the next issue?"

The girl groaned.

"Features. Lisa, couldn't you do anything better on the new German teacher? He can't be all that perfect. Doesn't he bite his nails or pick his nose or beat his wife or something? He just doesn't sound human." He shook his head and looked around at us. "When writing a profile, *dig*. Dig for the flaws as well as the good points. Everyone has them. You may not realize it, but even I'm not perfect."

"You're so right," Lisa said.

We all laughed. "The sports page isn't too bad. Matt's 'gorjus' prose perked it up a shade above its usual level. Now then, where're the new ideas? I've posted assignments for the next issue, but how about you guys coming up with some column ideas, features, whatever."

We all looked down at our hands or the newspaper, anything except at Dave. It didn't help. Then Halley raised her hand.

"How about that idea I told you about? The once-a-month Volunteer Opportunities column."

"Fine. Good. I thought you were working on it." He unexpectedly pointed to me, forgetting my name, as usual. "How about you?"

Put on the spot, you can imagine what happened. My face went on high burn, and I stuttered. "Well, uh, er . . ."

"Yes? Well what?"

"We have a lot of little stories about this club and that club scattered here and there. What if we, uh, put them all together under one heading and called them . . . I don't know . . . Club News? Clublicity? I don't know."

"Good idea. Yes." He studied me a moment. "You're uh, Carrie, aren't you?"

I nodded.

"Anybody else?"

After the meeting I checked the assignment board and found myself down for a story on the Chess Club. Bor-ing. What could you possibly say about chess?

I stayed as long as I could, hoping Matt would walk me home, but he and Lisa were talking over by the coffee machine, so I left.

A few minutes later, clanking down the iron steps of our school, I heard footsteps above. I waited a second on the second-floor landing, pretending to adjust my books. Matt came bounding down the last steps. "Well!" he exclaimed. "We've got to stop meeting like this."

I giggled, and the two of us started down the remaining stairs together. He reached behind him into his pack and pulled out an old book. "Remember Saturday? I was telling you about *Brideshead Revisited*? How the TV version differs from the book?"

What I'd actually remembered was how bright Matt's eyes became when he spoke about books and how good it felt when he held me on the dance floor.

"I brought the book with me. Thought you might want to read it. Evelyn Waugh was a remarkable writer. Really captured the British aristocracy. Showed the enormous influence of Catholicism on one family."

"She did?"

"*He* did. Waugh was a man."

"Oh." My goodness. Matt knew so much about books. "To tell the truth, what I liked best about the TV version was the love affair near the end," I said. "And it amazed me how the whole family stuck around day after day waiting for the father to die. Didn't they have any work to do?"

"You don't understand. People like that don't *do*. They just *are*."

"Oh." I took the book, touching the cover where Matt's fingers had been. "Thanks for this. I'll read it soon."

After that we didn't seem to find anything else to say. We'd reached the first floor and were heading to the exit. Our footsteps echoed in the empty hall. The exit door was just ahead. Once through it, we'd each go our separate ways. I glanced up at Matt and wished he'd put his hand on my back, like he did when he led me to the dance floor. He looked straight ahead.

"I liked your story a lot," I said to keep the conversation going. "The way they boxed it on the page made it look really important."

Matt shrugged. "It wasn't much."

"You must be thrilled with your first by-line."

"It's not like getting a story into the *New Yorker* or *Atlantic*."

"Oh no, of course not," I agreed. I'd never read the *Atlantic,* and the only time I looked at the *New Yorker* was in the dentist's office. And then only to read the cartoons. We were almost out the door. If he was going to ask me out, it better be soon. *Ask me. Ask me,* I willed silently. *Hurry!*

Matt pushed the door open, and we were outside. "Well, here we are," he said, blinking into the bright light. "The parting of the ways."

I shifted my books again and pushed my glasses up. This was it. Good-bye.

"You like basketball?" he asked, out of the blue.

"It's okay. I like it better if I'm playing."

"The Aztecs are playing our team Friday night. I have to cover it for the *Chronicle*."

Was he asking me out? "They are? Are they a good team?"

"Third in the league."

"No kidding!" Was third in the league good or bad?

"Doing anything Friday night?"

"Why?" I asked before my head sent out the startling news that Matt was asking me out.

"You could come along. We could get a pizza later."

Oh wonder, oh joy! He *was* asking me for a date! And then I remembered Bill and the magic interview. That was Friday night.

"I can't," I said, really disappointed. "I'm really sorry." Maybe I should have told Matt about the interview, but I didn't want anyone on the *Chronicle* to know yet. What if I made a big mess of it?

Maybe I wouldn't ask the right questions or there wouldn't be enough of a story, or I couldn't write it well enough. "I'm sorry, but I'm busy."

"Oh, right. It's pretty late notice."

"Yes." For another moment we just stood there facing each other, not knowing how to say good-bye. I could tell Matt felt awkward, embarrassed, like he could hardly wait to get away. Then, Lisa came out of the building with two other staffers. She nodded at us and went on towards the parking lot.

"Guess I better be getting home," I said finally.

Matt nodded. My bike was chained to a post in the opposite direction from the parking lot. When I looked back a few moments later, Matt had caught up to Lisa and the others. I waited until they all had left the parking lot before I got on my bike to pedal home.

"Carrie!" It was Mom's voice, a stage three. "Come in here!"

I jumped up from Lynn's dressing table, where I'd been examining a zit that was just beginning to show on my chin, and ran.

Mom was in the kitchen, tearing lettuce into a bowl. She pushed the bowl aside and wiped her hands on a towel. "Where are the potatoes?" She pulled the oven door open and stood aside.

"Potatoes?"

"Yes, potatoes! The schedule says you were supposed to get out five potatoes, wash them, and put them up with the chicken. Why didn't you?"

"I'm sorry, Mom. I forgot." What was wrong

with Mom? She never got angry over something so small.

"Did you set the table?"

"Not yet. I'll do it now." I started gathering plates and silverware.

"Car-rie!" This time it was Lynn's voice.

I didn't answer. Moments later she appeared at the kitchen doorway holding a scrunched-up piece of rainbow-colored something like it was diseased. "Look at this, Mom! I could murder her. She put my new sweater in the wash with Pam's red jumper, and then she baked it in the dryer for at least an hour! Just look at it!"

"Carrie . . ." Mom said in disgust.

"She's making a big thing out of nothing," I said. "Just wash it again in a little bleach and the color will come right out."

"In bleach?" Lynn screeched. "You stupid creep! You've lived in this world for fifteen years and haven't learned a thing! You still don't know about separating colored clothes from white?"

"If you don't like the way I do the wash, do it yourself."

"Who asked you to wash my things? Who gave you the right to go poking around my stuff? It wasn't even dirty!"

Uneasily, I slipped into the dining room with the plates and started setting them out. Lynn's sweater did look awful, all stuck together with static electricity and streaked with red. I hadn't thought. When I got home, I just gathered up whatever was lying around, like Mom always does, and threw it in the machine. Somebody had to do the wash. I didn't have a single pair of panties left. Nobody ever told me how long to run the dryer, so how should I know? But I knew I should have. It was the same sort of thing other girls seemed to know at my age—like putting on eye makeup.

"You owe me! I paid $30 for this sweater!"

"Try to collect."

"I'll get you, you . . . four eyes!"

"Mom!"

"Stop it! Stop it immediately," Mom cried. Tears glistened in her eyes.

"Hey, what's going on here? World War Three?" We hadn't even heard Daddy come in, and there he was suddenly, coat still on, watching us.

"Your daughters are at it again," Mom said, face white. She turned away.

"You know what she did, Dad?" Lynn started.

"I don't want to hear. Now come on. Just quit it. I come home from work tired and hungry and don't want to hear you girls screeching at each other like wildcats!" He took off his coat and left it on a chair.

"Please hang up your coat," Mom said quietly without turning around. "Or did you expect me to do it?"

Dad threw Mom a nasty look and picked up the coat.

"I'll hang it for you, Dad," Lynn said.

"No thanks. I'll do it myself."

Pam burst into the room and flung her arms around Dad's middle, nearly tripping him. "Daddy!" she squealed. He pushed her away.

"Pam, go wash your hands!" I ordered crossly. I took her roughly by the arm and walked her to the bathroom.

Later that night as I lay in bed, I thought about all that had happened before supper. Ever since Mom started working, things seemed to have gotten worse. She's tired every night, and I don't think she really likes her work. We all have to be careful around her because you never know what will set her off. Tonight was typical. Because of her mood we were all at each other's throats. Kind of like a pecking order—the big picking on the next biggest and so on down the line. I'd even picked on Pam, which made me feel really bad. She's just a little kid.

What was happening to us all?

Chapter Nine

I settled down next to Gayle on the school bus, tired and grumpy the next day. Worrying about what was happening to our family had kept me awake until late. Then, when the alarm went off I thought I'd stay in bed just one more minute. When I woke again, it was really late. I just had time to dress, slap two slices of bread over some cheese, and get Pam off to school.

"I don't like Mom's working," I said. "It's got the whole family out of whack. She says we need the money for college. But Lynn's only in junior college, and that hardly costs anything. Just books and spending money, which she earns herself, anyway. It'll be three years before I go to college, so why do we need the money?"

"It's not money," Gayle said.

"No?"

"Well, figure it out. How much could your mother be making? It's just a starting job, right?"

"I don't know, around four dollars an hour I think."

"Okay. $160 a week. Subtract social security and

withholding tax and medical insurance and she probably takes home maybe $120, if she's lucky."

It sounded like a lot to me.

"You forget about clothes and bus fare and a sitter for Pam and lunches."

"She could brown bag it. I do." Come to think of it, all the big ideas I'd had about fantastic lunches if I made them myself hadn't developed at all. I usually threw together the fastest things I could find.

"Brown bag it downtown? Are you kidding? If she wants to be one of the girls, she'll go out to lunch with them. There are dozens of nice restaurants. Figure at least $25 more a week. So, add it up. It hardly pays to work."

"Then why does she do it? We all hate it. The house is always a mess. There are never any clean clothes to wear. I couldn't find anything in the fridge this morning for sandwiches except this dumb cheese. It's awful, Gayle. I used to love coming home after school. Mom would be there and we'd talk. Now, there's only Pam. And a long list of things I'm supposed to do."

"Welcome to the club."

"No thanks."

"My mom says her working is good for us. She says we're learning to be self-sufficient. It's building character, she says."

"Yuch."

"Well, think about it. Before, your mother did everything."

"That's what mothers are for."

"Why? As much as I hate cleaning the kitchen and bathroom, my weekly job, I realize Mom did it for at least fifteen years. Who says she has to do all the dirty work for the rest of her life?"

"Her mother did it for her."

"Your mom's a college graduate, Carrie."

"I know," I said. Everything she said was true. The only thing was, with Mom working, home was the pits.

"Besides," Gayle said, looking away.

"Yes?"

"Marriage isn't permanent anymore. We women have to learn to take care of ourselves."

"My parents are *not* getting divorced."

"I didn't say that. Just be prepared, that's all."

"I don't want to talk about it!"

"Don't. But just remember, I'll be—"

I put a hand over her mouth. "Nothing bad's going to happen. It's all my fault, anyway. If I'd remembered about the potatoes, if I'd left Lynn's sweater alone, if I hadn't talked back, my parents wouldn't have argued."

"Car-rie!" Gayle cried behind my hand.

"No. Not another word." I took my hand away. The bus was pulling into the school grounds. Some of the cheerleaders were doing cartwheels or practicing dance steps on the front lawn for the basketball game tonight. They looked so pretty and alert and full of pep. I felt so grungy and tired and sad.

What do you wear to a meeting of magicians? Jeans or a dress? I settled for a pleated plaid skirt in shades of violet and pink, a pink sweater, and flats and hose. I washed my hair and fixed it almost as nicely as Lynn had. I put on eye makeup, a little blusher, and some lip gloss. With glasses on, I still looked like plain old Carrie.

The excitement of going to the scout meeting with Bill had drained away once I knew I could have been out with Matt instead. By now, I figured, Matt had probably asked someone else to the game. Probably Lisa. Maybe he'd never ask me out again.

"You're such a worrier," Lynn exclaimed when I told her that. "It'll do him good to think he has some competition."

"But he doesn't!"

Lynn groaned in disgust. "You are so naive, Carrie! I don't know what he wants with you in the first place."

"But it's not a game. I want to be truthful. Why should I pretend to be what I'm not?"

"Because men like 'mystery.' They also want what they can't have, or think they can't. Keep 'em guessing. That works all the time."

"Is that how you got Jay?"

"Jay and I went through that stage. Now I can be more up front with him. Sometimes, though, I make up little white lies, just to keep him off balance. You know . . ." She smiled coyly. "I talk to some guy and Jay sees us. I tell Jay the guy asked me out. No harm done."

"That's gross," I said. "It really is." And yet, deep down, I knew Lynn was right. The way I'd acted at the party proved it. Even though I hadn't lost the Ping-Pong game on purpose, if I'd won, I'd have lost. Know what I mean? And, feeling

beautiful—because of the way Lynn fixed me up—
made me act differently. More feminine, kind of. I
didn't jump in with opinions like I do at home. I listened a lot, wide-eyed and admiring. Part of that
quietness was due to the glasses, of course. Without them, I couldn't hear as well either. I don't
know why, but you use your eyes to read faces—
and faces help you understand what people say.

Anyway, Lynn was right. Boys like girls to be
just the way I behaved Saturday night.

Bill arrived a few minutes before seven-thirty
dressed in a black suit, the kind you see actors on
TV wearing when they're going to the Oscar
awards.

"My goodness," I said in surprise. "If I'd known
it was so formal, I'd have put on a party dress.
Where are we going?"

"No sweat," Bill said. "This is my costume.
We're going to an Explorer Scout Magic Show.
I'm trying to move up from Enchanter to Thau-
maturgist."

I slipped into the VW beside him.
"Thaumatur—what?"

"Thaumaturgist. It means a worker of magic."
Bill started the engine. "We start out as Sorcerer's
Apprentice. After we meet certain requirements,
like making our own wands, we move up to Sorcerer. From there, it's Conjurer, Enchanter, and so
on. There are eight stages before you can become a
full-fledged Magician. I'm a little more than half
there."

I took a small notebook from my purse and tried

to scribble what he was saying as we drove. I asked him to go over the eight stages and spell some of the words.

"How did you get started?" I asked.

He chuckled. "It was really funny. I knew a few card tricks other kids had shown me. One day I was taking a film back to the school library, and the kid who checked it in had a deck of cards. So I said, 'Wanna see a trick?' He said, 'Sure.' So I showed him the trick, a real simple one, and he says, 'Nice. Now, want to see one I can do?' "

For a few moments Bill had to pay attention to driving, then he said, "This guy, he starts doing all these fancy flourishes and fans and sleights of hand and I felt like an idiot. I asked him how he learned all that, and he told me about this scout troop dealing in magic. So, I started coming to meetings."

When we reached the building where the scouts were meeting Bill parked and we went inside. He took me to a small room with a stage, led me to a chair in front and gave me a program. "I have to get ready for my act, Carrie. Do you mind?"

I felt a little strange, all by myself, but I kept busy writing notes. The room filled up quickly with relatives and friends. Against the walls stood glass cases with all sorts of trophies and pictures of people holding their awards.

Finally, the lights went out and a spot lit the stage. A guy about my age walked out to stand in front of a table. Circus-type music played in the background while he held out his hands to show they were empty. Then he turned them down and up again. Out of nowhere a ball appeared in each

palm. He turned his hands down and up again.
Now there were two balls in each hand, and then
cubes, and then everything disappeared.

The acts got harder. One scout held up a single
scarf, ran it through his hands and it became two
scarves, then three. The scarves changed into a
rabbit. He put the rabbit into an empty box and
closed the box. When he opened the box, the rabbit was gone!

Most of the time I sat like a little kid at a birthday
party, grinning, eyes wide. After a while I tried to
spot how the tricks were done, but I could never
figure out how. The guys would talk as they did
their tricks and sometimes they were really funny.
The truth is, it was just magic!

Towards the end Bill came on stage. He looked
tall and distinguished and very at ease. "Has anyone got today's *Times* by any chance?" he asked. A
pretty girl trotted onstage and handed him a newspaper. He held it up and opened it to show that it
was in perfect condition.

"Now, I'm going to prove that you can tear this
paper into a hundred pieces and put it completely
together again. No glue or Scotch tape or anything—except magic. May I have a volunteer?"

A lot of hands went up. Bill seemed to be looking around the room for just the right person. Then
he pointed to me. "Will that pretty young lady
please come up to the stage for a moment?"

Flustered, I left my notebook on my seat and
hurried up the steps to the stage. I felt very self-
conscious and scared.

After he introduced me to the audience he gave

me a page of the *Times*. "Now," Bill said, "please do as I do. We'll each tear these sheets in half, then in half again, and in half again and so on." As he spoke he began ripping the newspaper into shreds. I followed his example.

"Now, young lady. Will you roll all these pieces into a tight ball and place them in the palm of your hand, like this."

I did as he told me. He did the same.

"Abracadabra Shish Boom Bah!" he said. "It is whole. Right?"

I shrugged. "I guess so." I grinned at the audience, meaning to say, "He's crazy, but I'll humor him."

"You say it's whole?"

"If you think so."

"Then open your hand."

I opened my hand, and of course all the little scraps of paper flew out to the floor. I started to laugh in embarrassment.

"Oh, my. Something must have gone wrong." Bill looked puzzled and concerned. "Or has it?" He opened his hand. Inside, just as in my hand, was a balled up wad of paper. Only his paper wasn't in shreds. He unfolded it slowly. The paper I'd seen him tear up just like I had was completely whole. It was a miracle.

You could hear the audience sigh in awe, and then they gave him a wonderful round of applause. Bill bowed very formally. Then, offering his arm, he escorted me to the stairs. "See you later," he whispered. "You were great."

"*You* were!" I whispered back. "Really!"

On the way home Bill said he used to get help with his acts. "Now I try to figure things out by myself. Half the fun is inventing something new. I'm working on a trick to stretch someone to nine feet tall."

"What fun!" I laughed. "How did that trick work where they put all the swords into the box the woman was in?" I asked.

He wagged a finger and said magicians never tell.

"You're so confident. I mean, you were really in control up there in front of everyone. I would have died."

Bill said he used to be very shy. "When you learn to do something well, you gain confidence. Did I tell you about my nutty German professor act?"

"No, what?"

"I used to do an act for kid shows, hair spritzed out to here." He held his hand five inches from his head. "Beard that goes off in two directions. Glasses hanging off the shnoz, tuxedo that's ten times too big . . ."

I shook my head in amazement.

"What I learned from that act was that I had to be myself. I created a real, crazy, mixed-up character, but part of him was me. It's important to be real, not phony."

When Bill walked me back to the house, I thanked him for a marvelous evening. Then, impulsively, I stretched up on my toes and gave him a quick kiss on the cheek.

"Oh!" he exclaimed, startled. He put a hand to the spot I'd kissed. With a look of surprise he pulled a small, red candy heart from his face. With a grin of sheer bliss he popped the candy in his mouth and put a hand over his heart. I laughed until I cried.

Chapter Ten

For the rest of the weekend I worked on the story for the *Chronicle*. I wanted to put the excitement of the show and Bill's fun and enthusiasm into words. It just wouldn't do to write something boring like "Bill is interested in magic; he took me to a magic show; some of the performers did this or that." Words like those sounded dead.

I spent a long time and a lot of thought writing and throwing away before I came up with the first paragraph, the lead. "Can you swallow a sword? Juggle five balls at once? Eat fire? Cut a woman in two and put her together again? Bill Westkopf can." That sounded pretty good to me. Once I got the opening, the rest of the story almost wrote itself.

I could hardly wait to reach school to see how Dave and Lisa would like it. Maybe I'd even show it to Matt, before Journalism, I thought.

"Have a good weekend?" I asked Gayle on the bus Monday.

"Terrible," she said.

"Why? What happened?"

"I went to the basketball game with Karen and Jane Friday night, remember? I told you we were going. Guess who asked me out for Saturday?"

"Robert?"

Gayle nodded, and her face glowed. "He's so much fun, Carrie. He's such a nice guy! We hardly watched the game, we talked so much."

"What's terrible about that? You've been hoping he'd ask you."

"Right, but what good is it? I couldn't go. Dad's house is thirty-five miles away. Do you know what that means?"

"So, Robert has to get you. Does he have a car?"

Gayle picked at a string on her worn notebook. "His car gets twelve miles to the gallon. That's three gallons of gas each way, not counting what it takes to drive to a local movie. Eight dollars, at least, not counting the movie!"

"Couldn't you stay with your mom some weekends?"

"Are you kidding? Have you any idea how it is after a divorce? Daddy says, 'The kids come to me, no excuses.' Mom figures she's in charge all week, so weekends belong to her. Last weekend she and Ned took a trip."

"Oh, gee, I'm sorry, Gayle." I put my hand on her arm. "Couldn't you have stayed alone, or stayed with us."

"I asked. I begged. I threatened and cried, but all Mom said was, 'Sorry, dear. We made these plans weeks ago and can't change them. You can't stay alone; it wouldn't be right. And maybe you can stay at Carrie's another time.' " Gayle imitated her mother perfectly.

Robert got on the bus and Gayle turned her head aside so he wouldn't see her tears. "How will I lead a normal life if all my friends are at school and weekends I'm miles and miles away?"

"Gayle, it'll work out. They have to understand. And maybe you'll make friends where your dad lives too."

"The youngest man I've seen on the block is my father!" Gayle said bitterly.

After that we didn't talk much until we were almost to school. I thought about my parents and how much arguing was going on and hoped, again, they wouldn't divorce. Then I asked Gayle the question I'd been wanting to ask as soon as Gayle had mentioned the game. "Was Matt there?"

"Yeah, I saw him," she said, very busy all of a sudden getting her books and lunch together.

"Did you talk to him? Was he with Robert or anyone else?"

We squeezed into the aisle and pushed along with everyone else. When we finally got off the bus I repeated the question.

"Robert hung around with me and Karen and Jane most of the time," Gayle answered.

"Gayle! Tell me! If he wasn't with Robert, who was he with? He said he had to cover the game for the *Chronicle*."

"Look, I've got to get to homeroom. Mrs. Cooper goes bananas if we're late."

"He was with Lisa, wasn't he?" I asked, suddenly sure. "Is that what it is?"

"Well, yeah," Gayle finally admitted. "But I wouldn't worry. They weren't together all the time."

Beverly Gannon took over as Lady High Commissioner of Etymology. It was such a relief to sit there, just another student, with my blood running quietly through my veins for a change. My only regret was that I had no excuse to face Matt anymore. Still, I felt his presence as if he actually sat in the seat behind me.

"Today," Mr. Hawkins said, "I'd like to talk about interview techniques. By Friday I expect each of you to write your first interview feature."

Oh boy, I thought. You've got the jump on everyone. Wait till Hawkins sees the neat feature I wrote on Bill in the next issue of the *Chronicle*. I dug around in my pack for a pencil and remembered it was back on my desk at home. Carrie, the forgetful.

"Once you've made an appointment to interview your subject," Hawkins said, "you need to do some research. What can you learn about the person before going to the interview? What kind of business is he or she in? What kind of work does he or she do? You can't ask intelligent questions unless you know something about people and their work."

Oh-oh, I thought, biting the borrowed pencil. I didn't know the first thing about magic before I went to that show with Bill. Maybe I should have taken out some books on the subject. At least I should have known something about the Explorer Scouts.

"It's a good idea to tape your interview," Hawkins said. "Most subjects don't mind and get used to the tape recorder in a few minutes. When you tape you get accuracy. You can quote directly. When you take notes, you're looking down at the notebook, not at the subject. You miss facial reactions. You lose eye contact. And of course, unless you take shorthand, you can't write fast enough."

Oh-oh, another booboo. I'd gotten so involved with watching the show I'd hardly taken any notes. When it came time to write, I'd relied on memory. Who knows how many mistakes I probably made!

"Questions," Hawkins went on. "You should have a list of questions ready before going to the interview. Other questions will come to you as you listen. But *listen*. Don't interrupt the answers and talk about yourself."

The more Hawkins talked, the worse I felt. The story I'd dropped off in Lisa's box just before coming to Journalism had to be awful. I'd winged it. I hadn't done most of the things Mr. Hawkins said a good interviewer should do.

As soon as the bell rang I scooted for the door. If I could reach the *Chronicle* before Lisa picked up the story, I'd go over it again at home. It was bad enough to be new. I certainly didn't need to be laughed at or cut down for sloppy work.

Matt and I reached the back door of the room about the same time. In my hurry, I didn't even notice we were heading for a collision.

"Hey! You on the track team too?" I think he grinned at me.

I say think because at that moment nothing else mattered except getting to the *Chronicle* office fast. I practically stampeded over him to get away, and I sprinted down the hall with just one thing in mind.

The office was closed. Locked. I peeked through the glass to the mailboxes. My story was still there. All I could do was glare at Lisa's mailbox and will my story to fly through the door into my hands.

For the next few minutes I stuck close to the office hoping that someone with a key might come by. All that did was make me a nuisance as I got in the way of kids changing classes. Then the bell rang for second period and I had to run.

I checked again lunchtime and worried through all the rest of my classes. It would be awful starting out with a bad story. I could just imagine Lisa giving it to me while everyone sat around listening— and pretending not to. By last period my over-active imagination had decided that the story was so cutesy that I'd be laughed right off the paper. I just had to get it back before Lisa read it.

"Sorry, uh, er, Carrie," she said when I caught her. "I picked up my mail third period and left it in my locker. I take the stuff home to read. You did make yourself a copy though, didn't you?"

Another dumb mistake.

"Well, don't worry. I never lose anything. I'll bring it in tomorrow, and then you can rework it any way you want."

Relieved, I turned to go. That's when I noticed the little white envelope in the mail cubbyhole near my name. Mail for *me*? My pulse picked up speed. My name was taped just above the hole. "Does that mean my box is above or below the name?"

"Figure it out yourself," Lisa said in an irritated tone. "There aren't any other names in that row, so it has to be yours, right?"

"Oh, right." I'd done it again, spoken before I thought. I grabbed the envelope and hurried out of the room. I didn't even look at it until I was far away from everyone. Could it be from Matt? I wondered. But why would he write me if he could talk to me in person? Finally, off by myself, I opened the envelope and took out the folded sheet.

This above all: to thine own self be true.
And it must follow as the night the day
Thou canst not then be false to any man.

Will

Oh, my! How beautiful. How philosophical! But what exactly did it mean? Who could have sent it—and why?

It was signed Will. Will? William? Bill! Bill must have written it! I thought back to our evening together and remembered what he said about finding his true personality so he wouldn't be phony. How romantic. The first time in my whole life that a boy wrote to me, and such a poetic thought (even though the words were kind of old-fashioned).

I could hardly wait to get home. I'd phone him, tell him how very neat his poem was, and ask him what he meant by it.

I dialed his home number three times, hanging up each time before the phone rang. It felt strange, calling a boy. I know girls do it all the time. Once I was at a party and the girls were looking up boys' phone numbers and calling them. They'd say things like, "Do you have Prince Albert in the can?" When the answer was "hunh?" they'd giggle and say, "Well, let him out."

"Bill," I greeted, shyly. My tongue seemed to be stuck to the roof of my mouth.

"Well, yeah. Hi. This Carrie?"

"Yes, how did you know?"

"Magic." I could imagine his grin. "So? How's it going? You finish that story yet? Gonna let me read it?"

"Yes, but . . ."

"Yeah?"

"I want to look it over some more. You know, make it really good."

"That's great. Will you show it to me soon?"

"Sure." I hesitated. "Uh, Bill? I want to thank you."

"Oh, don't thank me. It was nothing, really."

"Oh yes it was. It was beautiful. So thoughtful of you. It means a lot to me."

"It meant a lot to me, too. It's not every day I can share what I love doing."

How marvelous. Not only did he love magic, but poetry, too. "Bill? I just wanted to ask why you used those strange words. It's not the way we usually talk."

"Abracadabra?"

"Hunh?" For a second it didn't make sense. Then I realized my mistake. "You know something? I think we're talking about two different things. You're talking about the magic show, and I'm talking about the note you sent me."

"What note?"

"You know, the one about being true to yourself."

"Hunh?"

"You signed it, Will."

"Hunh?"

"You didn't send me a note?"

"No, Carrie, but I'd be glad to. In fact, close your eyes, and I'll send it by mental telepathy."

"Oh, no! I'm so embarrassed!"

"Well, just a minute. If you find that message too strong I'll send another. Concentrate."

"No, Bill. Stop joking. I feel just awful."

"Come on, Carrie. It can't be that bad. If you got a note from someone named Will about being true to yourself, then some guy must really like you."

"I sure don't know who. I don't know anyone else by that name!"

By the time we hung up we were laughing about it, but I was really puzzled now. If Bill hadn't sent me that note, who had?

Chapter Eleven

"Look at this, Lynn, will you? What do you think?" I asked, giving the note to Lynn when she got home.

She glanced at it. "Nice. Who sent it to you."

"Will. Didn't you see the signature? Whoever that is."

"Oh, you little dunce!" She started laughing, doubling over, covering her face, she thought it was so funny. I felt really hurt. When she finally stopped, she had tears in her eyes. "You are so illiterate! Will wrote it, all right. *William*. William Shakespeare! It's from *Hamlet*. Oh, Carrie!" With that, she went off in another spasm of laughing.

"You don't have to act so smart," I cried, wishing I could fall into a hole and never come out. "I bet you didn't know any Shakespeare at my age, either."

"Oh, that's so fun-ny!" She shook her head in disbelief. "Wait till I tell Jay!"

"Oh, shut up!" I grabbed my books and stalked out of the room. It's impossible sharing a room with someone like Lynn. She always makes me feel so dumb and ugly. When she gets really nasty, like now, I have to get away or we'd get into a fight. And I'd promised myself to control the urge to kill so Mom and Dad wouldn't get mad.

The only place in the house where you can get some privacy is the bathroom at the end of the hall. That's where I usually hide when I want to get away from everyone to think. I just close the door and sit on the bathmat with my back against the tub. I write poetry, or in my diary, or just read— until someone comes banging on the door.

A wave of excitement passed through me. It had to have been Matt who sent that note. I read the words again and again, imagining him holding the pen, wondering what his thoughts could have been. I'd treasure that note for the rest of my life.

Halfway down the hall, just as I passed Mom and Dad's room, I heard loud voices. I slowed down, then stopped. They were quarreling. I hate eavesdropping, but I do it a lot. You can pick up some of the juiciest news about people by listening to more than one conversation at a time.

"You mean to say you took our savings out of the bank?" Mom said in a voice close to hysteria. "You took money we saved, because I scrimped and did without . . . and didn't tell me!"

"Come on, Marian. Don't make such a big thing out of it." Dad's tone was playful, hearty, but strained. "It wasn't like that at all. I was going to tell you, but I figured to wait a bit. You know how cautious you are about money."

"With good reason!"

"There you go again!"

"Just how long did you figure on waiting before telling me?"

Dad gave a short, embarrassed laugh. "Well . . . It seemed such a terrific deal, Marian. Double your money in six months, the guy said. And I wasn't the only one. Everyone in the firm put something in."

"You were conned, that's what. And you won't even admit it. In five minutes you were sweet-talked out of money it took me fifteen years, *fifteen years* to save!" Mom sounded like she was close to tears. "I'm just beginning to realize it. I'm the workhorse, and you're the driver. My opinions never count. That's how it's been all through our marriage."

"Oh, come on. Don't generalize from one mistake. There just wasn't enough time to go to you. The real estate syndicate had to have the funds that day or lose out on this terrific investment. If I hadn't come up with the money, someone else would have!"

"How much do we have left?"

Dad cleared his throat.

"How much?"

In a low voice Dad said, "A couple of hundred. I'm not apologizing, mind you. If you don't gamble sometimes, you don't win big."

"And if you gamble and lose?"

Dad didn't answer.

"I don't like you, Al. I haven't for a long time," Mom said softly. If she'd screamed, somehow it would have been better. "I don't like what you've done to me, or to our family. And it's not just the money."

I didn't want to stay to hear any more, but I couldn't move.

"The feeling's mutual!" Dad exclaimed. He slammed something down. "I'm sick to death of your complaining. I'm sick of a lot of things around here!"

At that point I couldn't stand it. I didn't want to hear another word. Instead of going on to the bathroom, I turned and ran back to my room.

"Lynn!"

My sister looked up from her desk. "Hey? What's wrong?"

I pointed back down the hall, unable to get the words out, then flopped down on my bed and started sobbing. Lynn came to sit beside me. She put a hand on my arm. "Hey, what is it?"

In bits and pieces I told her what I'd just heard. She listened quietly, then got up and brought the tissue box to me. "Poor Mom," she said.

"Poor Mom? Poor Dad, you mean!" I whispered so we couldn't be heard outside the room. "She was the one who started it all. It's only money. Did she have to talk to him like that over just a little money!" I began to shake.

"Daddy shouldn't have done that, spent the money, without talking it over with Mom first."

Of course she was right, but at that moment it didn't seem to matter. "I'm scared, Lynn. The things they said. What's going to happen to us?"

"I don't know, Carrie. It isn't good."

"Do you think they'll get a divorce?"

"I don't know. I really don't." She seemed as upset as I was.

"Oh, Lynn. What will we do?" I cried.

She put her arms around me and let me cry. Neither of us had an answer.

"Maybe it was just a fight," Gayle said when she heard the latest. "Sometimes a good argument clears the air, and then they're okay for a while."

"Do you really think so?" I asked hopefully.

As usual, we were seated beside each other on the school bus for the half-hour ride. Sometimes I'd get so involved in what we talked about that I wouldn't even notice who got on or where we were until we got to school.

"Sure. My parents argued a whole lot before they finally called it quits. And actually, I was relieved when Dad finally left. Every time they fought I'd get so tied up inside I could hardly think at school."

"I remember."

"And now it's not too bad. I'm not crazy about Mom's kid boyfriend, but I'm learning to live with him. We stay out of each other's way, mostly. And if I look at the positive side, he has some points in his favor."

"Like?"

"Like he's good at math, and you know what a struggle I'm having with it. Mom's great with arithmetic, but give her an equation and she thinks it's Rubik's cube. I really hate asking Ned for help, but well, he noticed and he's been pretty good about it." She smiled. "In fact, I'm kind of getting to see what Mom sees in him."

"Gayle!"

"Well, gee, Carrie. I'm closer to his age than Mom!"

It didn't exactly relieve my worries to know that Gayle was beginning to adjust to her parents' divorce. In fact, what happened last night hung over my day like a black sky. What if tonight Mom and Dad announced they were separating? I loved them both. I didn't want to have to choose between them. I didn't want anything to change at home. It was tough enough finding out who I was and how to handle being grown up without the complication of our family breaking up!

Seeing Matt in Journalism, I thought for a moment of going up to him to ask about the note, but my heart wasn't in it. Somehow, I felt so sad and scared inside about things at home that being in the same room with Matt didn't do a thing. I sat through Journalism a zillion miles away. I sat through History and Math and Social Studies the same way. Any confidence I'd ever found in myself seemed to have disappeared. Every doubt was back. I felt terribly lost and alone and scared.

After school I *almost* went straight home. With Mom working and things so out of whack at home, I felt a need to be with Pam. I wanted to get her home, sit down on the couch with my arm around her and read a book together. I wanted for us to kind of hole up against the world.

If I hurried, I could make the bus back. Then I remembered that Lisa had promised to bring in my story. So, before going downstairs, I hurried over to the *Chronicle* office to get it.

Matt was there, and for a second my heart did that funny fluttery thing it does whenever I see him. But I didn't speak to him because I couldn't stay. The story wasn't in my mailbox. I asked if anyone had seen Lisa. Then, just as I started to leave, she came in.

Halley was tagging on her heels, just like she tags on Dave Roth's. I wondered if that was the way to score points with the editors.

"Yes, you can bring it in Thursday, Halley," Lisa said, picking up her mail. "No, I don't want to hear all about it now. If you're looking for more work to do come up with an idea of your own." It seemed to me that Lisa created an energy field when she came into a room. I could see why Matt liked her.

"Lisa?" I interrupted softly.

"Oh, Carrie. Yes. Just a minute."

Halley followed Lisa to Dave's desk. "What about the Dear Halley column? I think it would be terrific," she said, still at it.

"Halley, please! Leave it alone, will you? That idea's as old as the hills." Lisa turned to me. "I want to talk to you about that magic story."

Oh-oh. Here it comes, I thought. Another nail in the coffin.

Matt was watching us. I could feel my face begin to burn. Obviously, Lisa had read my story, and now she would tear it to shreds right in front of everyone.

"Sit down." Lisa pointed to the chair I'd sat in

on the first day I came to the office. She sat on the edge of Roth's desk, making her higher than me.

"You wrote this?" She held out my story.

"Yes."

"Without help?"

"No! I didn't have help! I mean, yes." I tried to keep my voice low so everyone in the office wouldn't hear.

"Well, I'm really surprised."

"Oh, I'm sorry," I said. "I thought it wasn't ready; that's why I asked for it back."

"Oh? You think so? Well, I don't," she said.

"Carrie, it's good. It has style. You packed a lot of entertaining information into a short piece. You gave us insight into a guy we all see every day and never thought to interview."

"I did?" I put my hands up to my face to hide how hot it was getting.

"You're surprised? You didn't know it was good?"

"Well, I, you see—Mr. Hawkins lectured on interviews yesterday, and I didn't do any of the things he said to do."

"That's okay. Rules are made to be broken. If you're good enough at something, you don't need to follow the rules."

"Well . . ." I glanced around. Matt, Halley, and two other reporters were watching and listening. I could hardly stand it, I was so happy.

"If you didn't know how to write a feature interview because Hawkins hadn't explained it yet, then I'd say you have some very natural talent. I'd like to see other things you do."

"Well, uh . . ."

"I liked the Clublicity idea you came up with, too. We're going to try it. You keep up the good work and maybe we'll turn it over to you."

"Oh wow!" was all I could manage to say.

She marked up the top of the page and handed it to me. "Give me a headline for this, and we'll go with it next issue. You'll note that I marked it for a by-line."

"Gee, thanks!"

"Nice work." She hopped off the desk and went to the coffee pot, already forgetting me. Matt's eyes met mine. He smiled. And then Lisa asked him something, and he turned away.

When I left, Halley was at one of the typewriters working, and the other two reporters waved goodbye to me, then went back to whatever they'd been doing.

Chapter Twelve

Lisa's praise warmed me somewhat and carried me through a busy afternoon. Pam and I cleaned the kitchen together, drank hot chocolate together, and read a book together. But at dinner, I sensed the coming disaster in the looks on my parents' faces. To stave it off I babbled on nonstop, with almost desperate speed, about anything and everything that came into my head. Mom and Dad played with their food, but you could tell their minds were elsewhere. When I finally ran out of words, Lynn gave me a look as if to say, "At last."

For a few minutes, or hours—it felt that long— nobody said anything. Lynn kept her eyes on the food. Pam pushed the beets aside with one finger, and Mom did nothing to stop her. I chewed the stew until it lost its taste. When I swallowed, it stuck in my throat like a rock. At last Daddy put his fork down. "Your mother and I want to talk with you girls about something. I guess now is as good a time as any."

I clenched my hands under the table trying to

think of something, anything that would stop him. But it was no use.

Dad smiled at each of us, tenderly. "First, you know, don't you, that no matter what, your mother and I both love you very much. Each of you."

My legs started trembling, and I pushed my fists down on them. Pam was pouring Bosco into her milk without measuring. Mom didn't seem to notice.

Dad waited a moment for his words to sink in. Then he said, "Now comes the hard part. Your mother and I have decided to separate. We've had some serious problems lately, and we think it would be better if we lived apart for a while."

"Does that mean you're getting a divorce?" I blurted.

"No, Carrie. We don't know about that yet. We hope we can work things out."

"Can't you do that without moving out, Daddy?" It seemed to me that Dad's actual leaving would make it harder for him to come back.

Mom and Dad exchanged looks. "We think it's best this way," Mom said.

"Why? Was it anything we did? Was it because Lynn and I fight so much? Is it because I'm so sloppy that you have to work harder, Mom? I'll change. I promise. I already have, a little. Is it because—"

Mom wouldn't let me go on. "No, Carrie honey. It's none of those things. It has nothing to do with you children."

"Then why?" I was so close to tears I had to bite my lip to stop them.

"Sometimes two people just stop loving each other. Stop caring," Mom said.

"Sometimes people love each other, but they're no longer in love," Dad said.

"What does *that* mean?" Lynn asked, speaking for the first time.

"It means," Dad said patiently, "that the special something which makes you want to be together is no longer there."

"Garbage!" Lynn exclaimed rudely.

We all looked at her.

"Garbage!" she repeated. "You're not sixteen anymore. You can't expect to be 'in love' like teenagers when you've been married for twenty years. If you say you still love each other—"

"Lynn, that's enough!" Dad said.

"You can't possibly understand," Mom said.

Lynn glared at them. Then she threw her napkin down, pushed her chair back, and left the room.

"Please don't do it," I begged, wiping away the first tears.

Mom got up and stood behind my chair. She bent over to touch her cheek to mine. "Honey, it will be all right. I promise. Your life won't change that much."

"I don't want Daddy to go away!"

"Where is Daddy going?" Pam asked.

Nobody answered her.

"Carrie honey," Mom said, taking the chair Lynn had sat in and reaching for my hands. "I know it hurts a lot, but it's painful for us, too. You must realize we didn't decide this overnight."

"I don't care how long it took." I pulled my

hands away and stood up. "Take more time. Think some more! It's stupid! You can't do this to us!"

"Carrie! You're acting like a child!" Dad said.

"So are you!" I didn't want to hear another dumb word. My parents were always telling Lynn and me that no matter how we didn't get along, blood was thicker than water. Whether we liked it or not, we were sisters; therefore we were supposed to love each other. Garbage! We never chose to be sisters. If they couldn't work out their differences—even though they had chosen each other—how could they expect us to work out ours?

I stomped out of the room just as Lynn had and went back to our room. My sister lay sprawled across the bed on her stomach, hands propping up her head. I plopped down on my bed, and we stared at each other.

"You know what I think?" Lynn asked.

"What?"

"I think Daddy's having a mid-life crisis. Maybe he's playing around. Mom should hold on until he outgrows it."

"She's too angry."

"She has a right to be. Have you noticed how he treats her? Like she doesn't exist."

"Maybe the job will make a difference."

"That's a dumb thing to say."

I thought about it a second, then said, "No it's not. If she gets to like what she's doing and people at work respect her for being good, she'll feel better about herself. Feel more confident. And then . . ." I couldn't believe it. Lynn was actually listening as if I made sense. It rattled me to see her so attentive. I almost lost the thought. "And then," I repeated, "uh . . . if she feels better about herself, Daddy would find her more interesting. When you're confident, I think people want to know you more."

"Carrie. Sometimes you amaze me," Lynn said, without the usual sarcasm.

"It's more complicated than that, I'm sure, but it might help. I mean—" I searched for words to express the half-baked thought. "I mean, if Dad respected Mom's opinions in the first place, he'd never have gone ahead and invested that money without asking her, would he?"

Lynn nodded, very interested. It was the closest she had ever come to saying I might be right.

"What can we do?"

"Nothing. Just hope, I guess."

We talked together in hushed tones for over an hour, something we rarely did without arguing. We talked about the fun we used to have as a family, when we were young: going to the zoo, having picnics, vacationing at the beach. We seemed to need to go over all the good things that had happened in the past because it would never be that good again.

During our conversation, though, we were both aware of the sounds outside our door. At one point Pam, complaining, went off to bed. Soon after, Mom and Dad's voices rose in a brief argument, then the outside door slammed. We looked at each other, then went on talking.

Afterwards I lay down on my bed, hands under my head, and stared up at the ceiling. All that emotion must have knocked me out because I fell asleep. When the phone rang at about nine-thirty, I awoke immediately.

Lynn brought the phone in from the hall, expecting it to be Jay, I suppose. "Hello? Yes. Just a minute."

She held the phone out without a word.

"Who is it?"

"A guy. Matt somebody."

Oh, no, Matt! I jumped to a sitting position, instantly awake. I smoothed my hair and wet my lips as if he were in the room. What could he be calling about? My heart started hammering so loud I was afraid he'd hear.

Lynn covered the mouthpiece with one hand. "Want me to go outside?"

"Please."

She picked up the book she'd been reading and quietly left the room.

I approached the phone as if it were a dangerous snake.

"Hello?" I said softly.

"Hi, Carrie?"

"Yes."

"This is Matt. Matt Baldwin."

"I know."

"I called to congratulate you on that story you wrote. Lisa let me read it, and it's really good."

"Thanks."

"Heard her talking to you and I wanted to say something, but I turned around for a second—and the next thing I knew, you were gone."

"I had to go home."

"Carrie? Hey, is something wrong? You don't sound like yourself."

I couldn't take it. He sounded so full of concern that it was like a pin pricking the big bag of hurt in my chest. Horror of horrors—my face got hot, and my glasses steamed up, and the tears started running down.

"Carrie?"

I covered the mouthpiece so he wouldn't hear me. Then I hung up.

A moment later the phone rang again. By the third ring I had things under control.

"Carrie? Matt. Are you okay?"

"I'm sorry, Matt. I hardly ever cry. It's just that everything kind of got to me. My parents told us tonight that they're going to separate, maybe divorce."

"Gee, that's tough. I'm really sorry." He paused. "Want to talk? I'll come right over."

I sniffed and wiped my eyes with one hand. It was too late, and I didn't trust myself to talk about it to him yet. I'd only cry again. "No. Thanks though."

"Are you sure? You sound like you could use a good ear. I've been known to be a good listener."

"No, Matt. I'm sorry I laid it all on you, but I'll be okay. Other kids survive. Guess I will, too." How brave I sounded, considering how I felt.

I could imagine Matt looking at me with those serious, probing, dark eyes. I could imagine him taking me into his arms and letting me lean against his chest and cry. But I didn't really know him well enough yet for that.

"Carrie? Do you know this one? ' "I weep for you," the Walrus said, "I deeply sympathize." With sobs and tears he sorted out those of the largest size, holding his pocket handkerchief before his streaming eyes.' "

"What?" When the words sank in I realized what he was saying. It was from *Alice in Wonderland.*

"Now that sounds more like you!"

"Thanks, I needed that," I said. I could feel his grin through the telephone wires.

"See you tomorrow, Carrie. Take care."

Chapter Thirteen

I saw Matt way down the hall. He was leaning against the wall near the Journalism classroom, reading. Instantly my pulse picked up and my face got hot. Could he be waiting to see me? By the time I reached him my heart was really pounding, and the wet palms of my hands stuck to my books.

"Hi, Carrie." He closed the book and detached himself from the wall.

"Hi," I returned. Though I felt a bit more cheerful than last night, a heavy uneasiness still clung to me. Daddy had left and not come back. This morning, Mom's note on the breakfast table had said nothing about last night, yet everything. Carrie: Please do the usual before school, and if you have time, vacuum before getting dinner. We'll have muffin-pizzas tonight. Fix the salad, shred the jack cheese, and toast eight muffins. I'll do the rest." She signed it with love and added a P.S.: "You've been wonderful, honey, helping so much. It means a lot."

I'd felt pleased by Mom's appreciation. She didn't often find good things to say about me. But then, the significance of "eight muffins" dawned. Daddy wouldn't be eating with us—she'd have asked me to toast ten. That realization had turned me cold.

As the memory returned now, the same coldness returned. "Got a minute?" Matt asked. "Let's walk down the hall a bit." He put a hand on my back and steered me along beside him.

"How are you doing?" he asked softly.

"Okay." I swallowed, determined not to go into the whole long story. It would only bring back all the hurt. "Well, not so okay really. My dad didn't come home last night." I looked up at Matt and felt tears blurring my eyes.

"Look. If it's any consolation, probably fifty percent of the kids at school have gone through or are going through what you are."

"Small consolation."

"Knowing you, you'll come out okay. You'll probably make something good of the experience."

"Yeah, like writing a feature on how kids survive their parents' divorce, maybe."

"There! See? What did I tell you?"

"Oh Matt. I didn't really mean that. I couldn't. Not now, anyway. It hurts too much."

We'd reached the end of the hall. Mr. Hawkins came towards us. "Hey, you two!" he greeted. "Aren't you going the wrong way?" He strode by us on his way to the classroom. Matt and I turned around and made our way back.

"Matt? Did you send me that note from *Ham-*

let?" I asked just before we went into our room.

"Ah! You recognized the quote!"

I couldn't disillusion him by telling the truth—that it was Lynn who recognized where it came from. I just nodded. "I'd like to ask you something about it some time."

"How about today, after school? Meet you in the *Chronicle* office, okay?"

"Well, okay!" We smiled at each other and went to our seats.

Not until last period did I remember about the Chess Club. They met only once every two weeks on Thursdays. If I didn't check on them today, Thursday, it would be two weeks before they met again. Roth would think I didn't want to do the assignment. But I was supposed to meet Matt after school. Maybe, I thought, I could see him before going to the club meeting and ask him to wait half an hour or so.

Halley sat at Roth's desk, feet up on an open drawer, a *Mad* magazine in one hand and a doughnut in the other. I said, "When Matt comes in, could you tell him I forgot that I have to cover the Chess Club? I'll be back in about half an hour, if he can wait."

"Sure," Halley said. "If I'm still here."

"Oh, then, never mind." I rummaged through my notebook for some paper and scribbled a note. "I'll just put this in his mailbox. Thanks anyway."

"Anytime," Halley said, taking a bite from the doughnut.

* * *

"There's not much to tell about our club," Roger Cannon, the head of the Chess Club, said. "Ever play the game?"

"Uh-huh, but I'm not awfully good at it. It takes being able to plan ahead, and I've never been much good at that." I laughed. "I'm lucky if I can work out my next move without losing a piece."

"Actually, chess is very exciting. It's a lot like plotting a battle. You have to be a good strategist. We've got some really good players. Beverly and Jonathan are competing in the finals at State next week."

"Really?" I took notes, making sure to spell the first and last names of Beverly and Jonathan correctly.

"Feel free to watch and ask questions," Roger said, and then he wandered off to get a game going for himself.

Actually, watching chess being played is kind of boring. Not much happens. All the players do is lean over a board and stare at the pieces without talking. Then, after a long time, someone finally moves a piece.

As I walked about, I tried to figure what would make news. The fact that two players from our school were competing at the finals made a paragraph, maybe, but that's all. What else could I do with the Chess Club? Could I somehow use Roger's point about chess players being good strategists? Maybe I'd try an editorial comparing the game of chess with planning careers.

When I got back to the *Chronicle* office Halley was still there, alone. This time she sipped coffee and was reading the assignment board.

"You see Matt?" I asked.

"Matt, yeah. He was here a little while ago, left with Lisa."

A big disappointed lump grew in my throat.

"We had some excitement here. Dave broke the news that Lisa's taking over his job when he graduates in June. You should have seen the fuss. Matt went out and brought back a bottle of ginger ale. We pretended it was champagne and toasted the big lady Editor-in-Chief. Lisa loved it. She ran around and kissed all the guys."

I felt like asking, Matt too? But of course he'd be included. In fact, the whole reason for the kissing might have been to kiss him. I felt so badly at having missed the fun and even worse that Matt left with Lisa. Swallowing my hurt I asked Halley if she had told Matt what I said.

"Tell Matt? No. You left a note, didn't you?"

The note lay in his box. Had he read it? I decided no. With all the excitement, he'd probably forgotten all about meeting me. Maybe it was time to stop daydreaming about life and face the realities. I'd hurried away from Chess Club so I wouldn't keep Matt waiting—and he had gone off with Lisa, not even leaving a note. All those fantasies—about walking hand in hand, going to school dances together, talking endlessly, kissing sweetly—were dumb, just as dumb as the deep-down-in-my-heart dream that Daddy and Mom would get together again. The real truth was cold and simple: Matt liked me as if I were a kid sister, and Mom and Dad would never patch up their differences.

With those heavy thoughts I left the *Chronicle* office. Better get my bike and get home to Pam. Life at home was uncertain enough without upsetting her more by being late.

Pam and I were just settling down to some cookies and milk when Lynn came home. She hardly ever got home before five, so I was really surprised. Without saying a word she marched into our room and closed the door. I left Pam drinking her milk and promised to let her help with dinner.

Lynn lay curled up on her bed, eyes closed, arms crossed over her stomach when I came in.

"Lynn? Are you okay? Are you sick or something?" I asked.

She opened her eyes and stared ahead with the saddest look I'd ever seen. I sat opposite her on my bed, watching.

"I broke up with Jay."

As much as I didn't like loud, boastful Jay, I was sorry. To Lynn he was handsome, exciting, open, ambitious, and warm.

"Why?"

Lynn closed her eyes. "I thought he was an original, but he wasn't. He's a fake. He used me as a straight man for his jokes. You were right about him. A lot of noise and very little substance." Lynn's voice broke, and she took a deep breath.

"But what happened?" I moved over to her bed and put an arm around her. "Lynn? What happened?"

"I tried to tell him about Mom and Dad," she said. "I just needed to get some—perspective—on what's happening. I don't know, I needed his sympathy, understanding—something."

"So?"

"So I'd hardly started telling him about last night when there was just a little pause, and then he started talking about guess what? Football! Comparing Mom and Dad's situation to a football game! Can you imagine?" Lynn gazed at me with wide, puzzled eyes. "I listened, not saying a word, trying—really trying—to see the point. But it totally escaped me. He went on and on about football, forgetting all about what I'd been talking about!"

"Was it an interesting game at least?" I asked.

"What?" She looked puzzled, then laughed. And then we both started laughing, not because anything was funny, but just because. When we stopped, Lynn wiped her eyes and said, "I realized that Jay never really knew who I was, or cared. He's so wrapped up in himself, he doesn't see anyone else."

"I'm sorry, Lynn. Do you think maybe he'll change? I mean, you do like a lot of things about him. Maybe you could teach him to *listen*."

"Not very likely."

I thought how little I liked Jay, but Lynn had found things in him that mattered. "Maybe you could still see each other, not as before, but . . . you always said he's so much fun."

Lynn shrugged, but she seemed slightly cheered at the thought.

"Do you think Mom and Dad could change, or are they too old?"

Lynn got up and went to sit at the dressing table.

She began to comb her hair. As I stood behind her our eyes met in the mirror. "What do you think?" she asked.

"I think that they have a lot at stake—twenty years of marriage and three kids. If they care enough and try hard enough, yes. I think they could change. The question is, do they care enough?"

Lynn and I stared at each other for a long moment, and then she turned around, stood up, and hugged me hard. I laughed in surprise and delight and hugged her back.

The four of us, Mom, Lynn, Pam, and I, ate dinner together without Dad. It would be that way, I supposed, for a while, maybe for always. I worried about Dad. He doesn't know how to cook. What would he eat?

Mom seemed in a good mood and told funny stories about the bank manager not being able to balance her own checkbook. Mom seemed to know what everyone at the bank did as if she were asking herself what position there might make her the happiest.

When Lynn told her about Jay, Mom said, "I never did think he was right for you, dear, but figured it would be better if you found that out for yourself."

Right after dinner, while Lynn and I were cleaning up, the phone rang. This was the hour Jay usually called. "You answer it," she said.

"What if it's him?"

"Tell him I'm out. It will do him good to think I'm not pining away for him."

"Lynn," I protested.

"All right, so tell him I don't want to talk to him. Not today, anyway." She wiped her hands on a towel. "That leaves the door open."

Expecting Jay, I answered jauntily. Now that I didn't have to be polite for Lynn's sake, I could say what I liked. But it wasn't Jay.

"Matt?" I asked, incredulous.

"Right. The guy in your Journalism class. The guy you were supposed to meet after school today. Did you stand me up?"

"I left a note," I said. "In your box."

"Oh no! I've got to get used to checking that box every day. I thought you'd forgotten."

"I'd never forget." I could have bitten off my tongue when I heard what I'd said. I rushed on with words tumbling all over each other about going to the Chess Club, trying to pretend I hadn't said that.

"So, that was it! I'm just a pawn in your life, not the king."

"Ooooh," I groaned, catching the pun.

"Did you hear about Lisa?"

That she kissed you? That you left the office together? "Yes! That's really great. She'll be a good editor."

"A bunch of us went off to the coffee shop to celebrate. Too bad you weren't there."

"I wish I had been." A bunch of them? Halley hadn't said others went off with Lisa and Matt.

"Hey, are you busy tonight? I'd like to come over and we could go for a walk."

"Well, sure."

"Okay. Be right there."

Flustered, happy, I hung up. Lynn pushed me off to the bedroom to get ready. In a few minutes she came back in. "Better wear my new down jacket; it's starting to snow."

"I may sweat it up. I might get a stain on it," I said.

"You do, and I'll make hamburger out of you!" She checked me over critically. "Want me to fix your hair? Want me to do your eyes?"

Should I? Should I go without my glasses? Oh, I felt so nervous! "No," I said. "To thine own self be true and all that."

Ten minutes later I walked out the door with Matt. It was really cold, with snow swirling around the lamplights. Matt pulled the sheepskin collar of his jacket up and dug his hands into his pockets. I tugged the yellow knit cap down over my ears and stuck my tongue out to catch the snow. Without a word we fell in step together and started down the street.

"Why did you sent me that passage from *Hamlet*?" I asked.

"To thine own self be true . . . ." He grinned. "Don't you know?" His gray-green eyes twinkled knowingly.

"Tell me."

He took my icy hand in his. "Cold hands, warm heart." He put our hands into his pocket. It was the first time in my life that a boy had done that. I felt so—connected, and now I tried hard to keep in step with his long strides.

"Want the truth?"

"Of course."

"All of it?"

"You're scaring me."

"I bet. You love it."

I giggled. "Tell me."

"Okay. In the beginning, I thought you were the most exciting Lady High Commissioner of Etymology our class ever had."

"Matt! There have only been two this term so far, me and Randy!"

"Oh, really?" He pretended surprise.

"Matt, come on! Stop teasing."

"Okay. What did you want to know?"

"Just what did you mean by 'To thine own self be true,' and all that?" Actually, I knew what it meant, but it seemed terribly important to hear it from Matt.

"If you really want to know, it occurred to me after we met at the party."

"What occurred to you?"

"That the Carrie I met there wasn't the true Carrie."

I puzzled about that for a second. "Who's the *true* Carrie?"

He stopped under a lamp and faced me, putting a cold finger on my lips. My whole body flamed up even though it was so freezing that every word we spoke came out in little puffs of steam.

"The true Carrie is cute, but kind of disorganized. Serious, but I suspect—since I don't really

know her well—full of the devil. Smart, resourceful, original . . . shall I go on?"

I grinned at him, sheepishly, absolutely delighted. "Keep going."

"You're kidding! No shame at all."

"What else? What else?" I tugged on his sleeve.

He grinned and took my hands. "The true Carrie
blushes when she's excited, and I like that because
she blushes a lot."

I blushed.

"And even though she wears glasses, she has the
biggest, most talkative eyes I've ever seen."

A big lump formed in my throat, and I looked
down at the ground. No boy had ever spoken to me
like that. *Nobody* had ever told me such nice
things.

Matt lifted my chin and smiled. "Carrie?"

I swallowed. "Yes?"

"Will you go to the basketball game with me Friday night?"

I almost said, "Matt, I hate basketball, unless
I'm playing," but I stopped myself. Instead I
asked, "Who's playing?"

"Does it matter?"

I giggled. "I guess not."

For a second we stood there in the cold, steam
filling the space between us as we breathed, and
then Matt drew me to him. He held me close, our
thick jackets like pillows between us, and I turned
my face up to him.

My glasses got all foggy, so I reached up, took
them off, and slipped them into my—I mean
Lynn's—jacket pocket. Then I grinned at him, shy-

ly, because I knew he was going to kiss me and I could hardly wait.

I closed my eyes as his face came toward me, then his lips touched mine. They just brushed me, almost like the feathery snowflakes, and I opened my eyes in surprise. But then he kissed me again, harder this time, and a little breathlessly.

From then on, I can't describe how it was because I just stopped paying attention and *felt*. I guess you could say it was like the very best of my daydreams, but better because it was real. My knees got weak, and my face got very warm—even though the temperature was below freezing.

When he pulled back at last, I kept my eyes closed awhile longer, smiling. I opened them to find him watching me and shaking his head. "Oh Carrie, oh Carrie . . ."

Usually, I would have said, "What do you mean?" But I knew what he meant, and for once I didn't ask the obvious. For a second I remembered Gayle's gift, the T-shirt with the words Writers Are Novel Lovers on its front. And I started to laugh. Next time I went for a walk with Matt, maybe I'd wear it.

When a teen looks for romance,
she's looking for

Caprice romances represent the finest in love stories written especially for you—today's teen! Filled with the challenges, excitement and anticipation that make romance so wonderful, **Caprice** novels deliver irresistible reading pleasure, month after month. If you enjoyed this book, treat yourself, or a friend, to the **Caprice** experience... just fill out the coupon below!

Send me:

I WANT TO MEET BRUCE PENHALL IN PERSON!

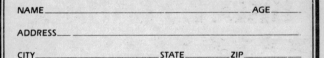

NAME_____ AGE_____

ADDRESS_____

CITY_____ STATE_____ ZIP_____

SEND TO
MEET BRUCE PENHALL CONTEST
CAPRICE
BERKLEY PUBLISHING GROUP, INC.
DEPARTMENT BW
200 MADISON AVENUE
NEW YORK, NY 10016

OFFICIAL RULES

Winner will be selected at random. No purchase necessary. (Alternate means of entry: send information above on a 3" x 5" card to MEET BRUCE PENHALL CONTEST.) Employees of MCA, Inc., and Sterling's Magazines, Inc., including subsidiaries and affiliates, and their families are ineligible to be contestants. Contest void where prohibited by law. All federal, state and local regulations apply. Winner under the age of 18 must be accompanied by parent or guardian. All travel expenses paid.

All entries must be postmarked by August 31, 1983.

QUESTIONNAIRE

NAME _____

ADDRESS _____

_____

AGE _____ GRADE _____ SCHOOL _____

In order to make CAPRICE Romances the best
romances for you, we'd like your opinion on teen
titles. Since you are helping us, we'd like to send
you details on our new, exciting CAPRICE Proof-
of-Purchase Gifts *plus* 6 Points towards your own
CAPRICE Special Gift.

1) How many paperbacks do you read in a
   month? _____

2) How many teen romances do you read in a
   month? _____

3) Where do you get your romance paperbacks?
   school library _____ public library _____
   school or magazine book club (which one) _____

   _____

   drugstore _____ bookstore _____
   grocery store _____ stationery store _____

4) Do you like any one line of teen romance paper-
   backs? First Love _____ Sweet Dreams _____
   Wildfire _____ Other _____
   I like them all _____

5) Do you have a favorite teen romance author?

   _____

6) What attracts your attention when you decide to
   buy a teen romance? title _____ cover _____
   information on back cover _____ author _____

7) What magazines do you read regularly? _____

   _____

8) What do you like to do in your spare time?

   _____

9) I found this questionnaire in the CAPRICE
   Romance entitled _____

Enjoy your CAPRICE Romances
and keep reading!

Please send this questionnaire to: Berkley Publishing Group
Department BW · 200 Madison Avenue · New York, New York 10016